THE NICKEL-PLATED BEAUTY

The last day of the month I was out in the barn with the other kids while Clarrie milked Ginty. All of us felt sad. It had just stopped raining that morning. Everything was still wet and cold outside, and we were thinking about how little time we had left and how we'd probably never be able to pay for the Nickel-Plated Beauty.

Clarrie looked up from her milking stool. "Maybe you didn't count right, Hester. Maybe we have more than you thought. Maybe we won't have to earn a whole five dollars and sixty-six cents."

I knew I'd counted right, but if they wanted me to, I'd take out the salt sack and count the money again right in front of them. Mama was busy in the house with Sarah, who was just getting over a cold, so the coast was clear. I took the board off Ginty's Hole and got down on my hands and knees to look inside.

Disaster struck once more! There wasn't anything in Ginty's Hole but dirt! The white salt sack was gone!

I let out a yell that made everybody come running. "It's gone!" I told them. "Our money's gone!"

THE
NICKEL-PLATED
BEAUTY

Patricia Beatty

A Beech Tree Paperback Book
New York

1 3 5 7 9 8 6 4 2

Library of Congress Cataloging-in-Publication Data

Beatty, Patricia, 1922–1991.
    The nickel-plated beauty / Patricia Beatty.—1st Beech Tree ed.
        p.   cm.
    Summary: In the Washington Territory of 1886, the seven
resourceful Kimball children devote themselves to earning enough
money to buy their mother a new stove.
    ISBN 0-688-12279-5
    [1. Family life—Fiction.   2. Washington (State)—Fiction.]
I. Title.
[PZ7.B380544Ni   1993b]
[Fic]—dc20   92-27683   CIP   AC

To Clara Soule

and

to Ethel Ross Hickok

CONTENTS

CHAPTER 1

Rust

The old stove began to go on a Saturday morning late in April, 1886. One of the screws in the oven door had rusted, and it fell out when Mama stooped down to fetch the hot biscuits for our breakfast. She frowned as she came to the big round golden-oak table, where everybody but me sat waiting. I was to bring the country gravy over as soon as everybody had Mama's pale-brown biscuits on his plate, and then, after they had been split open and spread with home-churned sweet butter, I'd spoon the gravy over them. There was nothing Pa favored so much as biscuits and country gravy. He ate them every morning of the year before he went out with his team, wagon, and wood saw to cut timber for the railroad.

"Joseph," Mama said quietly, "there's going to have to be a new stove."

"Is it as bad as all that, Estella?" he asked, reaching for the butter.

"It's that bad. When a stove starts to rust out in this part of the country, it goes fast. We've had good service from that one, but we'll need a new one before long."

"I'll go see Jake Willard about it today."

Mama sighed and sat down between Sarah and Tom. She tucked in their napkins, buttered their biscuits for them, and motioned for me to come around with the big frying pan. Mama's face was sad. Her reddish-yellow hair was as neat as ever and her cheeks pink and pretty, but her rose-colored calico dress was faded, and even her cameo brooch couldn't hide the frayed edges of her collar. I wasn't going to have the rose-colored calico for a hand-me-down, after all. Come to think of it, I hadn't had much in the way of hand-me-downs all spring.

We Kimballs had never had much money. Now I knew for a fact that we didn't have any. That was what came of cutting wood for the railroad. Pa had the contract for the Oregon and Washington Navigation Company. He cut down the timber to be tossed into the locomotive fireboxes. Pa and his helpers, men he hired from all over the peninsula, worked hard, cutting and stacking wood alongside the track, but he didn't get paid until the railroad people came along and measured the wood. We never knew when they were coming, and they hadn't come in a long time. Until they arrived, there wouldn't be any money.

When the tides were low and the digging good, Pa and Whit and Cameron dug clams on the beach and sold them in Nahcotta, the nearest town. Sometimes we ate clams ourselves for days. We fell back on the ocean lots of times for clams and oysters and crabs and fish; it saved on the pickled meat Mama put down for us, but what we got from the sea didn't bring in very much money.

In 1886 there were seven of us Kimball kids. First came Whitney, who worked after school in Mr. Willard's general store. I came next. I'm Hester, the one with the good head on her shoulders. Then came Clarrie and Cameron, who were ten and nine; Anna, eight; Tom, six; and Sarah, who was the baby of the family.

Whitney had started work right after Christmas. He refilled the gumdrop, horehound, and peppermint candy jars in Mr. Willard's store. He kept the stock—calicoes and muslins and shoes—nice and clean and dust-free. Not that we worried much about dust at Ocean Park, which was right on the beach in Washington Territory. Rust was what we mostly worried about. And rust was what gave us all our trouble that year. I hate rust!

It was all because of being poor. Being poor is a bad thing, and I really minded it. Whit minded it, too, even if the rest of the Kimballs, the little ones, didn't seem to care. But Whit was thirteen and I was twelve, and we saw the rich summer people at the beach. They were so rich that they didn't care if the sand ruined their fine things. They'd just go home and buy more, if they couldn't get what they wanted at the general store. Sometimes they even had things sent to them from Portland.

As for us Kimballs, we had run up a bill at Mr. Willard's general store. Whit's dollar a week pay went on that big bill, but it couldn't whittle it down much. We always needed sugar, flour, lard, dried beans, or cloth, because we couldn't raise those things ourselves.

The day the stove began to go we ate breakfast in silence, and then Pa got up. "I'll go see Jake Willard right now. We'll get it over with," he said, wiping his moustache on his napkin. "I'll drop Whit off. Who wants to go along?"

All of us looked at our empty plates. Nobody liked Mr. Willard. He never gave out a peppermint or a chunk of horehound candy. He never gave us anything, not even when we paid off his bill.

"Hester will go," Mama said. "I need a card of pins—we can afford that—and a spool of white thread for my new quilt."

So I had to go. I put on my yellow muslin dress and my old sunbonnet with the rickrack around the brim, to protect my complexion, and went out on the big front porch to wait. Clarrie would have to do the breakfast dishes while Cameron worked the pump for her. At least, I'd got out of that.

In the yard the chickens were busy scratching and dusting their feathers in the sandy dirt. I heard them squawk and saw our Plymouth Rock rooster chase a bold chick in a flurry of little feathers.

Red and Jerry came nosing at my shoes as I stood with my arm around a porch post. Red was a long lanky dog, the color of a bay horse. Nobody knew where he came from. He just showed up one day at our back door. Pa fed him and he stayed on. He wasn't much account, except that he liked to go to the beach with us and try to bite the waves.

Jerry was a big black-and-white dog with thick, soft fur. He was old, looked tired, and had sad eyes, and, as Mama said, it was no wonder. Five of us Kimballs had learned to walk, hanging on to Jerry's fur. He had been given to us when he was a puppy by some summer folks, who got disgusted because he barked so much. Jerry was a real barker, but we were used to it. Pa said he was a good watchdog. We didn't really know about that, because nobody strange ever came calling.

Pa came from the barn soon, driving the black rig almost as if it was Sunday. Whit sat next to him. My brother's face was dark, and he was quiet. He didn't like working all day Saturday for Mr. Willard.

Pa looked good. He'd put on his brown coat, and wore a hat. As I got up over the wheel, he doffed the hat to me. "Seeing as how I was taking a lady on an outing, I thought I'd get spruced up a bit."

"You look fine, Pa," I told him. I knew why he was dressed up. He wanted to impress Mr. Willard.

Regent, the pretty little chestnut horse Pa had traded for, was in the shafts. After balking twice, he finally got going. Pa said he liked Regent's balking. He liked a challenge in a horse, and Prince and Maude, the big white workhorses, had lost all their challenge a long time ago.

Nahcotta was only a mile away. We could have walked it easily, but Pa wanted to show Regent off. We passed the six other houses and the dozen empty summer cottages that made Ocean Park a dot on the map of Washington Territory. Mrs. Johnson was hanging out her wash. Vestal and Virgil Johnson, who were Clarrie's and Cameron's ages, waved to us.

Bert Hogan, another neighbor, was walking over the dunes toward the beach. He had a shotgun under his arm, and called out to Pa, "Want to go snipe hunting today, Joe? Hear they's plenty of them about now."

"Got to go see Jake Willard," Pa called back.

Bert Hogan scowled, spit out some tobacco juice, and walked on. He had a bill at the general store, too.

Mr. Hogan was all we saw, and then we turned east toward Nahcotta. The sun was bright; the sea gulls circled above us, calling to one another and diving over the sand dunes. The morning smelled fine. The wild strawberries, growing in the sand, were in bloom. Their talcum-powder-white petals looked like small five-pointed stars. In late May or early June, if the weather held, there'd be tiny sweet berries no bigger than my littlest fingernail.

I could hear the sad sound of the buoy out at sea far in the distance, and I shivered. It did sound like a lost soul, just as Mama once told us. I liked the beach and the friendly dunes, but I was afraid of the ocean when it stormed. Even when it was calm, I was careful of the sea.

The crisp salt air made my brown hair curlier. The long ringlets tightened up, and pretty soon I knew they'd look like little corkscrews. I didn't like that. I liked long, soft, butter-yellow hair, but of course I didn't have it. We Kimballs were dark, every single one of us. We had Pa's curly hair and his brown eyes. Mama's pretty reddish hair and blue eyes never came down to anybody. It was disgusting. We knew that we were called "the glowering Kimballs" by some of the summer people, and although I didn't like the description much, I had to admit it fit. Whit was a real glowerer when he went to work.

Nahcotta was big. It had the general store,

Aunt Rose Perkins' Palace Hotel and Eating House, a saloon, a blacksmith's shop, ten houses, a couple of docks, lots of fishnets spread out on poles to be mended, and about sixty people. Nahcotta smelled of salty things—of nets covered with brine and of oyster shells and fish. The town lived off the oyster beds in the bay. Willapa Bay oysters were famous in fancy Portland restaurants.

As we went past the Palace Hotel, I began to wish we'd been in the old wagon. I wanted to scrooch down, so Mama's older sister, Aunt Rose Perkins, wouldn't notice me. I kept a close lookout, but I didn't see her red hair anywhere. You could spy Aunt Rose's carrottop a mile away, everybody said. Aunt Rose kept asking Mama to have me work for her in the summer. Mama had told me that if I ever did work for Aunt Rose, I could keep the tips I earned for my-self—even if we Kimballs did need the money. But I didn't want to. Aunt Rose had a mean, wicked tongue, and she slapped her hired girls when they did anything wrong. No hired girl would stay with her long; she'd had dozens of them and they all quit. I was scared of Aunt Rose.

I did see Uncle Cedric Perkins, her hus-band, though. He was on the steps of the general store when we drove up, a jug of coal oil in his hand. Pa called to him as he tied Regent to the hitching post. "Hey, Ced, how come Rose let you out alone?"

"Lamp run low last night. Rosie sent me," said Uncle Cedric, a little man with light-yellow hair and a wispy blond moustache.

Pa shook his head as Uncle Cedric walked off. Everybody in Nahcotta knew how Aunt Rose treated him. They even whispered that she had horsewhipped him once when he didn't do what she told him. And she wasn't any bigger than he was.

The three of us went into Mr. Willard's store. We didn't walk in very bravely, either. I closed my eyes the minute I got inside the door. There was only one thing about the general store I liked, and that was its smell. I liked the smell even if I was afraid of Mr. Willard. His store smelled of peppermint, leather harness, kerosene, pickles, fresh-ground coffee, and oranges—fruits that cost so much we only saw them at Christmas. There wasn't any other smell in the world like Mr. Willard's general store.

Whit darted out of sight like a scalded dog as Mr. Willard came up to us and leaned on the counter. His shirt had pale-blue stripes

and his sleeve garters were violet. When I
got close to him, I could smell the rose hair
oil he used. He was a tall, thin man, with
black hair combed over the top of his head
in strings, and long, shiny sideburns. His
skin was as yellow as the cheese in his glass
case, and his moustache was only a thinnish
black line. He had little black eyes.

"What can I do you for, Joe?" he asked,
in the same words he always used.

"I need a stove, Jake," Pa said. "Our old
one's gone to rust."

"What do you figure on using for
money?" Willard asked, looking warningly
at me as I eyed the jar of mouth-watering
brown horehound candy, sprinkled with
white sugar. "The railroad men come along
and pay you for your wood?"

"No, not yet," Pa replied. "Guess you'll
have to put it on the bill." Pa looked up at
the ceiling, where bits and traces, hames and
reins hung, as if he was mighty interested
in buying some new harness gear for our
horses.

"Can't do that, Joe," Mr. Willard said.
He laughed. His teeth were probably store-
bought. We had thought so for a long time,
but weren't really sure yet. They were as
long as Regent's and as white as Red's. No-

body else on the peninsula had teeth like that. "I ain't got a stove in the place, and don't intend to order one for anybody unless he can show me the color of his money."

"Want to swap a stove for a horse? Got me a good-looking chestnut outside," said Pa. He kept on looking at the ceiling.

"I got me a good horse and a good team for delivering orders. I ain't trading no horseflesh with you today. Now was there anything else you had in mind, Joe?"

I spoke up as Pa, red in the face, turned away. "Mama says she needs a spool of white thread and a card of pins."

"Help yourself, Missie," the storekeeper said. "Guess I can put them on the bill. Don't come to more than fifteen cents."

CHAPTER 2

The Wonderful Wish Book

When Aunt Rose saw us leaving the general store and hailed us, I almost begged Pa to drive Regent on. Aunt Rose was sweeping the hotel porch, and came right out into the street, waving her broom at us. Regent shied, while Pa tugged on the reins and yelled, "Whoa!" Then he bellowed at her. "Put that cussed broom down, Rose. You're scaring the horse. He's going to bolt."

Of course Aunt Rose didn't. She shoved the broom right under Pa's nose. "I want to talk to you, Joe Kimball. You've been avoiding me lately."

I tried to melt into Pa. Aunt Rose had her snapping blue eyes on me. I knew what she wanted. For two years she had said the same thing when she saw me, measuring me up and down each time. "My, my, Hester, you're getting to be a big girl, aren't you? You could do lots of work now, I suspect."

Now she said, "Good thing Cedric told me he'd seen you. Get down from there, both of you. Come inside and have a cup of coffee with us."

Pa sighed and calmed Regent down. Aunt Rose had won again. People were looking at us. Pa knew, too, that if we went inside, Uncle Cedric, even if he was a tattler, would have a few minutes of peace while Aunt Rose had somebody else to tear into. Not that she dared say very much to Pa. He wouldn't take it off her for long.

Pa fastened Regent to the Palace Hotel hitching post, and we got down. I kept behind him as close as I could. Aunt Rose led the way, of course, across the porch and past the rocking chairs, set out already for summer guests. A pail and a scrub brush stood in the middle of her potted plants in the empty parlor.

Uncle Cedric was on his hands and knees, and he looked up as we came in. He smiled at us, but spoke to his wife. "I was just getting to the scrubbing, Rosie."

"I can see that," she said sharply. "It can wait for a bit—long as it gets done this morning. I want to talk to Hester and Joe.

You can come to the kitchen, too, and have a cup of coffee with us."

He got up slowly and brought up the rear of the parade as we marched through the long dining room and into the big silent kitchen. A tall blue-speckled pot steamed on the back of one of the three cookstoves. I knew Aunt Rose's famous coffeepot. Everybody in Nahcotta knew her coffee. It was strong. Aunt Rose drank it without sugar or cream, and glared at anyone who dared ask for them.

Pa and Aunt Rose sat down. Uncle Cedric got out three cups and filled them. Then he brought me a glass of milk.

"I'll have cream and sugar, Ced," Pa remarked. He didn't fancy getting heartburn from Aunt Rose's coffee.

Uncle Cedric got a pitcher from the cupboard cooler and the sugar bowl from another cupboard. "Here you be, Joe," he said. "Lucky they were left over from the breakfast mush."

Aunt Rose cut him off. Her eyes, just the color of winter pond ice, stabbed into Pa. "A fine thing it is," she said loudly, "to make me run out in the middle of the street and drag my brother-in-law down out of his rig to have some sociable coffee with Cedric and me. Because of you, I had to go make a spectacle of myself."

I drank my milk in a couple of gulps to keep from laughing. Aunt Rose never did anything except make a spectacle of herself.

"Now, Rose," Pa said, soft as butter, "you know I work in the woods and don't get over to Nahcotta more than once a week. You said you wanted to talk to us. What's it about? I ain't got all morning."

"It's about Hester." She came straight to the point. I sat up and stared at the wall calendar behind her. When Rose Perkins looked at you, you felt as though she'd stuck you on a pin and thought you were a common-looking bug at that. "Now is Hester going to work for me this summer or isn't she?"

Pa took a sip of coffee. With the cream in it, it had turned greenish. "Well, I just don't know yet, Rose. Maybe Estella is going to need her around home. Tom and Sarah get to be a real handful in the summers."

They said that before her marriage Rose Whitney had been the prettiest girl in Oysterville, where she and Mama came from, but I couldn't see it—particularly when she got mad, and Aunt Rose was hopping mad now. She scowled. Her pointed

16

nose and pointed chin got red. Then she got up and, flouncing off in a rustle of black bombazine, slammed the kitchen door.

Pa and I got up. "If you ever get out our way, Ced—" Pa began.

But Uncle Cedric spoke up sadly. "Not much chance of that for a time, Joe. Rosie and I have the spring cleaning to get done before the summer people come."

Pa nodded and we left. I was still scared, though, and looked over my shoulder to see if Aunt Rose was watching, but I didn't see her. Then I remembered the stove. "What'll we do about a stove?" I asked.

"We'll just have to make do, I guess," he said, looking straight ahead as we drove out of Nahcotta.

I'd been afraid he would say that. We Kimballs "made do" a lot—a whole lot more than we liked.

Pa went on. "Wish we could buy Mama a new stove, but Jake Willard has the right of it, Hester. A stove's a big item to put on a bill."

We didn't talk anymore after that. There wasn't anything to say.

That night Whit brought the new Montgomery Ward catalog home with him, and after supper all of us crowded around the marble-topped table in the parlor, while Mama turned the kerosene lamp up as high as it would go without smoking. What a wonderful wish book it was! I blessed Mr. Montgomery and Mr. Ward for it. My mouth watered when I looked at the patterned surah Sunday dresses for girls—or rather, for "young ladies." Even though they only came in red or blue, they were still pretty. Mama's hand lingered over a page of crystal-silk morning gowns, but Clarrie sniffed at the dresses. She and Cameron gazed at bicycles for $17.45, grand bicycles, fit to ride on in Portland or Astoria. Anna wanted a Texas saddle for $13.95, while Tom and Sarah asked right out for shoofly rocking horses. Mama promised quickly that Pa would make them one this winter. We couldn't afford it just now.

Whit and Pa didn't look at the catalog at all. All evening my brother sat scowling in the ladder-back chair next to Mama's quilting frame. "Don't you want to see the wish book, Whit?" I asked.

"Nope," he replied. "I already looked at it."

Pa was out in the barn. He was doing something to Regent's hoof that might stop the chestnut from balking. I wasn't fooled much when he told us he didn't want to see the catalog. Mr. Willard's turning him down on the stove had made Pa sad.

The Montgomery Ward catalog went back to the general store the next morning. We talked about it for a long time and about all of the pretty things we'd looked at, but after a while we got onto other matters— like how fat our pig was getting and how much bacon and ham we'd have for winter and how many mice Willoughby, the big gray barn cat, was catching.

The kitchen stove seemed to be holding up. Pa put the bolts back in as fast as they fell out, and Mama didn't talk about rust anymore, although we all knew that once it got started rust never stopped in the salt air at the beach.

Everything was just the same, except for one thing. Whitney acted funny. He moped, he didn't have much to say, and he glowered quite a bit. He wasn't doing well at school, either, these days. Pretty yellow-haired Miss Jenny Pitchford, who taught all the grades from Tom's first grade up to Whitney's eighth all in a one-room schoolhouse, looked upset when he couldn't recite the multiplication table from the two's to the twelve's. He used to be able to do it. There was something wrong, I knew; something was on his mind.

It all came out one morning the first week in May when we started for school. Cameron and Tom complained to me that Whitney had talked in his sleep all night and had kept them awake. Whit looked pretty bad. He had dark circles under his eyes, and he was pale when he came to walk beside me. He didn't swing his lard-bucket lunch pail, either.

"I got to talk to you, Hester," he said, as we went by Pa's stacked wood. By now it was so high we couldn't look over it.

"Something's been bothering you, Whit," I told him. "What's it about?"

"The stove," he explained.

"It's holding up all right."

Whit shook his head. He needed to have Mama cut his hair. "I don't mean the old stove. I'm talking about the new one."

"What new one?" I stopped.

"The new one I ordered from the wish book."

I gasped at that like a gaffed salmon, and I guess I must have turned as pale as my brother. Then he told me about it. One day

Mr. Willard had made out a C.O.D. order to Montgomery Ward and had told Whit to seal the envelope and put the stamp on the letter. Whit knew something about C.O.D., because he heard the summer people talking about it. He remembered a lady saying, "C.O.D. is really a blessing when you don't have the cash handy. It's the quickest way to get anything you need delivered right away." Whit looked at the stove part of the wish book, where there was a picture of a Sunshine Stove, the fanciest and most expensive stove in the whole catalog. It was called the Nickel-Plated Beauty. He added it to Mr. Willard's order.

Mr. Willard's order had come through yesterday, and so had Whit's stove. Mr. Willard was surprised to find a cookstove with his order, and he had put two and two together and thought of Whit. He got the truth out of him right off, and when he found out what Whit had done, he fired him.

"Have you told anybody yet?" I asked.

"No. That's what I wanted to talk to you about, Hester. What am I going to tell Pa?"

"I don't know, Whit. He won't be mad because you tried to buy Mama a stove, but we need what Mr. Willard pays you pretty bad."

"I know we do. I sure wish I'd known what C.O.D. meant," Whit said, "but I guess I know now."

"What does it mean?" I asked him.

"Mr. Willard explained it to me without my even asking him. It means 'cash on delivery.' "

I gasped again. The information surprised me as much as it had Whit.

He went on. "The Sunshine Stove cost twenty-five dollars. Mr. Willard paid for it. He sure got mad, Hester!"

I guess I must have looked sick, because Clarrie came up to me and asked if I had a headache or something. "I don't feel sick. I'm thinking," I told her. "We're in real bad trouble."

"What about?"

Whit groaned. "Guess we might as well all know now." He called Cameron back from where he was walking on a rail. Tom, who followed Cameron everywhere, came with him, and in a minute Anna was there, too. Whit told the story again while all of us, even Red the dog, listened.

He told it fast, because we could see Vestal and Virgil Johnson walking the ties behind us. They were part Indian. The boys didn't talk much, but they sure listened a lot. They had a bad habit of walking up behind you, quiet as a cat. They made me jump out of my skin when they did that, but they didn't mean to scare anybody. It was just the way they walked. We didn't want them to know about this, though. When we had trouble, we Kimballs kept it to ourselves if we could.

"What'll Whit do?" Clarrie asked.

"I don't know what Whit will do," Whit said sadly. Red whined, and he reached down to rub his ears.

"I know!" Anna piped up. "We'll ask Miss Jenny. She knows all about everything. She'll fix it for us."

So that was just what we did. We waited until morning recess, and instead of going out to play, we went up, all together, to Miss Jenny Pitchford's desk at the end of the schoolroom. She was grading long-division papers, but she looked up right away.

"What's this, a delegation from the Kimballs?" she asked.

We didn't know what a delegation was, but we nodded. Miss Pitchford had smiled when she said it, and her dark-blue eyes had been friendly.

Then Whit told her all about the stove, while she looked down at her desk and played with her red pencil. She didn't say anything right off. She got up and picked up the old school bell. We waited while she walked to the door, her long piled-up yellow hair and her blue calico skirts bright in the sunshine. Miss Pitchford gave the recess bell a good long ring and then spoke to us. She was frowning. "I'm going to let school out a half hour early today, children. We'll all go visit Jacob Willard and see if we can't straighten this out."

We went, too, right after school, the seven of us, Miss Pitchford leading the way, the strings of her white sunbonnet flapping. She was fighting mad. I thought that was peculiar, because everybody on the peninsula knew Mr. Willard was courting her.

The general store was empty this late in the day, and Miss Pitchford, with us trailing behind her like a flock of wet chickens, went right up to Mr. Willard. He saw the look in her eye and us at her heels. I think he wanted to duck behind his counter, but she saw him first.

"I'd like a word with you, Jacob," she said.

"Nothing could be more pleasant." He grinned at her, trying to buy her off, I guess, but she wasn't having any of his sweet talk.

"Whitney Kimball has told me that he

ordered a stove for his mother C.O.D. and that you fired him."

"That's right, Jenny."

She pointed to us. "The Kimballs need the money Whitney earns. Have you thought of that?"

"The boy did a dishonest thing." Mr. Willard stood right up to her, even if she did have blood in her eye.

"Whitney did not know what C.O.D. meant."

"He knows now! Cash on delivery. He could have looked it up." He said it so loudly we all shivered.

"Jacob," said Miss Pitchford in a softer voice, "give the boy his job again, please. He's learned his lesson. He won't do it again."

"He sure won't. I wouldn't let him near an order again."

"Then he can have his job back?"

"Don't go putting words in my mouth, Jenny. Maybe if someone talked a little nicer to me, I'd be inclined to do something for Whit." He grinned at her again.

Miss Pitchford was quiet for a long while. She looked at the counter instead of at Mr. Willard. "All right, Jacob. He'll be back at work right away. But what about the stove?

What are you going to do about the stove?"
She wasn't through with Mr. Willard yet. I
held my breath.

"What do you mean—the stove? I'll sell
it. There's room in the storeroom for it.
Somebody'll want it pretty soon, bad as the
rust is here at the beach."

"The Kimballs need it."

"They ain't getting it. I can't put it on that
big bill of theirs, Jenny. Joe Kimball's got
to show me the color of his money for it."

"That's not what I had in mind—not right
now. What if you held the stove for a while
and let the Kimballs work it out?"

He shook his head. "I can't afford to pay
more than one Kimball at a time. I haven't
got jobs for a tribe like that."

I heard Clarrie draw in her breath. Sometimes Clarrie cussed, because boys cussed. I
stepped on her toe with my shoe. Things
were going along pretty well. I didn't want
it spoiled.

"Perhaps something will turn up that will
let them buy the stove. Whitney meant to
give it to his mother at Christmas. Can you
hold it until then?"

I drew in my breath. Miss Pitchford had
told a flat-out fib. Whit hadn't had any ideas
about Christmas at all. I don't know what

Whitney had been thinking about when he ordered the Nickel-Plated Beauty C.O.D. I think he thought it would be some sort of present to us from Montgomery Ward and that he could have Pa take it home in the wagon.

Mr. Willard thought for a while. "Yes, I guess so," he said finally. "I won't put it up for sale until a week before Christmas. That suit you, Jenny?"

"Yes, Jacob, it would."

"There's a square dance in Ilwaco pretty soon—" he began to say to Miss Pitchford.

But I didn't let him finish. I don't know what got into me then. Just as bold as brass, I spoke out. "Thanks, Mr. Willard, for giving Whit his job back. We'll pay for the stove, all right. Just don't tell Pa about it."

Jacob Willard wasn't pleased. "*Who's* going to pay for it, Missie?"

I went on like a spooked horse. All those months from May to December had gone to my head. "We kids will, Mr. Willard. We got a long time to do it in." I turned to my brothers and sisters. Their eyes were round as marbles and their mouths wide open. "Can we do it?" I asked. "We'll have to earn twenty-five dollars ourselves. It's a lot of money."

Clarrie said, "It's a whole lot of money."

"Aw, we can do it," Cameron bragged.

"Good," I said. "It's just like in *The Three Musketeers*. You know the part I read you—where D'Artagnan and the musketeers say, 'One for all, all for one.' "

Whit broke into a smile. One by one the others did, too. Mr. Willard threw back his head and laughed, but I didn't care what he thought. We'd show him.

Miss Pitchford looked surprised, and then she smiled at me like a sunrise. "Good luck, Hester," she told me.

CHAPTER 3

The Strange Summer Boy

Miss Pitchford and Whit stayed inside the store while the rest of us Kimballs went home. "How are we going to earn all that money, Hester?" Cameron asked me. "Pa doesn't make that much in a month most of the time."

"I don't know," I said. "But I know one thing: Whit can't help us—not with his working every day in the summer. If we're going to do it, we'll have to do it by ourselves. And there's something else, too. We'll have to keep it a secret."

"I like secrets," said Anna.

"So do I," said Tom.

"Well, that's a good thing," I told them, as we stopped in the middle of the sand road that led to our house. I wiped Tom's nose with a red bandanna. His nose was running most of the time, and it always ran worse when he got excited. "It's going to be a hard secret to keep. We sell raspberries from our bushes every summer. Now we'll have to make more money from them and keep it a secret. We'll have to work harder and get more clams than we did last year, too. And we won't be able to earn twenty-five dollars just from clams and raspberries. We'll have to do it some other way. You got any ideas?"

I guess I must have sounded like Miss Jenny, because Cameron put up his hand. "We can pick wild strawberries," he said.

Clarrie sighed. I knew why. That was real hard work. You could pick all day and have only half a lard pail full of them, they were that tiny, but everybody knew they made the best jams and preserves you ever stuck a spoon into. Our wild strawberries would sell. Even though the sand dunes were covered with strawberry plants, everybody hated to pick them bad enough to buy them.

Cameron was full of ideas. "There's other kinds of berries, too," he went on. "We can pick salmonberries in June, and in July and August we can pick wild blackberries."

"In September we can pick cranberries in

Mr. Ross's bog on Saturdays. He'll let us. He's real nice," Clarrie said. Clarrie would like that. Cranberries weren't squishy like the other berries when you grabbed too hard.

Anna spoke up. "We can go to the crab holes, too, early in the morning."

"I can fish off the dock at Nahcotta," Clarrie put in. She loved to go fishing.

"I can chase Bert Hogan's old Holstein cows home. They're always getting away from him." This last was Tom's nickel's worth. He was too little to chase the Holsteins, though; the rest of us would have to do it. But it wasn't a bad idea. Tom was going to be a thinker someday.

"We'll have to get our own cows, Jersey and Ginty, home first," I warned him. "You look after them, Tom. They'll come for you. We'll bring Mr. Hogan's cows. If you ran off chasing somebody else's cows, Mama might miss Jersey and Ginty. She'd wonder about it and start asking questions."

Clarrie was worried. "Will somebody tell Mama?"

I shook my head. "Not if we keep quiet. I don't think Mr. Willard will talk, and we know we can trust Miss Pitchford. We can start on Mr. Hogan's cows right away, but most everything else'll have to wait till the summer folks come. As soon as they get here, we'll go around to all the cottages and ask about berries and crabs and clams. Too bad it won't be the right time of the year for oysters. Maybe it's a good thing for us that Pa's too busy with the wood saw now to go clamming. This way he won't find out how many we dig."

Then I told them what I was going to do. It was a terrible thing I'd decided. "I'll go to work for Aunt Rose this summer. I won't have time to do much clamming or berry picking. That's going to be your work—even Sarah can help pick berries. Mama will get what wages Aunt Rose pays me, but we'll put the tips I get waiting on tables onto the stove. Mama and Aunt Rose both promised me the tips would be mine."

My brothers and sisters looked at me as if I'd just said I was going to go out in the barn and let Maude, the biggest of our work-horses, kick me.

"That's the bravest thing I ever heard," said Anna.

"Old Whit sure got us a peck of trouble, didn't he?" said Cameron. "It won't be much of a summer, working all the time."

I turned on Cameron. "Well, we got his

job back for him, didn't we? We're going to get that stove, too. The stove is for Mama. Whit won't say it ever, but he's sorry about this. He'd pay us back if he could, but his pay goes on our bill at the store. Just you remember that!"

My brother dug his toe into the sand. "What if we get the twenty-five dollars, and Mr. Willard skins out of the deal? What if somebody else gives him thirty dollars for the stove?"

"Don't worry. He won't sell it," I said grimly.

"How are you going to stop him?" asked Anna.

"We've got a witness. Miss Jenny heard him say he'd keep it for us." I thought hard. What I said was true, but what Anna and Cameron had said was true, too. Pa always said to get a thing in writing. "We'll make him sign something."

"In blood?" Cameron said.

"Well, maybe not in blood," I said, "but in ink, not in pencil. Tomorrow's Saturday, and we'll go see him."

"We'll look at that stove, too," Clarrie put in. "Maybe it's no good and we won't want it."

"All right." I started home, swinging my

empty lunch pail. It never once came into my mind that we could save up our money until we had enough and buy another stove then. This was the only stove I thought about. It was Whit's stove. "All you have to remember now," I told my smaller brothers and sisters, "is to keep quiet and not tell a soul."

"In blood," I heard Cameron mutter. He wouldn't ever be satisfied if Mr. Willard didn't at least use red ink.

I talked to Whit first that night out on the front porch in the dark, and told him what we'd said on the way home. Then I went inside, where Mama was making quilt blocks, and told her about my going to work for Aunt Rose.

Mama looked tired tonight. Her face was peaked against the shiny black horsehair of her chair. She sighted the eye of her needle against the lamp. "Are you sure this is what you want to do, Hester? I thought you didn't want to work for your Aunt Rose."

I lied. "I want to buy a dress I saw in the wish book." I really wanted the dress, but it would have to wait, so it was only a half lie. Half a lie was half of the truth.

"Very well," Mama said. "I'm proud of

your enterprise, Hester. I'm sure anything you choose will be in good taste. You have a good head on your shoulders."

I held my breath and uncrossed my fingers behind my back. It had been easier than I'd thought it would be, and I'd thought it out carefully. Aunt Rose Perkins was the only answer I could think of.

After the little kids had gone to bed, Whit, Clarrie, Cameron, and I made up a paper for Mr. Willard to sign. We used a pen and a bottle of ink with a label on it that said *Never Fade* and we made our paper ironclad. We put a dotted line at the bottom where Mr. Willard could sign. The rest of us would sign it, too.

The next morning all of us, except Sarah, went back to the general store with Whit. We went right up to Mr. Willard and put our piece of paper under his nose. Whit spoke for us. "We want to have it put in writing, Mr. Willard."

Mr. Willard put on his gold-rimmed spectacles—he didn't wear them most of the time—and read out loud what we'd written down. It didn't sound as elegant as it had last night when I read it to Whit and Clarrie and Cameron. "Afraid I'll sell your stove out from under you?" he asked us.

We didn't say anything. We just looked at him—six of us Kimballs. We must have been too much for him. He took a pencil from behind his ear and started to sign his name. "No, you have to sign it in ink!" I hollered.

Mr. Willard wasn't happy about it, but he got out his ink and pen and put his name down on our dotted line. We all signed, too. Now we had his promise in writing.

Then Mr. Willard took out another sheet of paper from under the counter and wrote fast for a minute. He grinned and shoved his paper at us. "You kids are bound up by this here contract, just the way I am, you know. You might think better of it later on."

Whit read what Mr. Willard had written. "We, the undersigned, promise to pay to Jacob Willard the sum of two dollars for storage charges on one Sunshine Stove on the date of its purchase, twenty-seven dollars to be paid in full by the end of the third week of December, 1886."

"Twenty-seven dollars!" Cameron burst out. "The stove costs twenty-five dollars!"

"It's fair and proper," Mr. Willard said. "The stove takes up space in my storeroom."

"It doesn't either," Whit argued.

"Don't really matter. What I say goes. It's my storeroom."

We signed Mr. Willard's paper, and we made him promise to keep the whole thing a secret. He agreed to that. Mr. Willard thought he had won the day, but when I asked him if we could see our stove, he couldn't say no to us, although he'd have liked to. He had to let us all go back to his storeroom, and we went alone. We couldn't steal anything as big as a kitchen stove.

Proud as punch, Whit led the way; he'd unpacked the stove yesterday. We crowded around to look at it. It was a real Nickel-Plated Beauty, all right. Most of it was as shiny and pretty as black silk. The rest of it was fancied up with silvery nickel curlicues. The oven door had "Sunshine Stove—The World's Finest" spelled out on it in nickel-plated letters.

"Boy, it'll sure brighten up the kitchen," said Clarrie.

Tom whistled. "It's really worth twenty-five dollars."

"How would you know, Tommy?" said Anna. "You can't count that far yet. You only got up to fifteen last week."

"Put a blanket over it, Whit," said Cameron. "It might get rusty, too."

Whit opened and closed the dampers. They didn't squeak a bit. He lifted the lids to show us how fine the stove was on the inside. Then he took out two little cans and held them up. "They came with it," he explained. "Montgomery Ward sent them. One's Black Satin Stove Polish. The other's Nickel Silver Polish. I'll keep the stove clean, you bet! We won't need a blanket."

We were impressed that two polishes had come with the stove. It was nice of Montgomery Ward to send them.

Then Mr. Willard stuck his head in the door and asked if we were going to be back there in the way all day long. I wanted to stick out my tongue at him, but the stove wasn't ours yet. We had a long way to go to earn the Nickel-Plated Beauty. We scooted for home, but I had Mr. Willard's paper in my dress pocket and Mr. Willard had our paper folded up in the bottom of his cash drawer.

May passed. Bert Hogan paid us a penny each time one of us brought his cows home. We didn't make much from that, of course, but we hadn't expected to make anything until school was out and the summer folks had come.

In the meantime, we hung onto our secret. We didn't tell Sarah anything really; she was too little to know what we were going to do. We did tell her she'd have to pick berries with us this summer, and she thought that was just fine.

Miss Pitchford didn't talk about our agreement with Mr. Willard. We heard that she went to the square dance at Ilwaco with him and that she hadn't smiled as much as she usually did. We heard, too, that she didn't wear her best dress, either.

After Memorial Day came the end of school. Our summer had started. Now we waited for the summer people to arrive. The elderly Peterson sisters from Astoria came first. Then came the Addisons. Their little girl had red curls and whined all the time. She hated us, because we let her hold a clam once and it squirted in her eye. Next came the bunch of real old people from Portland. There were five couples, and they'd come to our beach every summer as long as Mama could remember. After that the other people came. We didn't know their names yet, because the rest of the cottages were rented to different people each summer.

Finally, by the middle of the second week in June, only the biggest, finest house of all, the Benton place, was empty. We worried about the Benton Place. The Bentons were the best customers we had had for our raspberries last year. They had lots of company from Astoria, and they ate lots of shortcake. Whit and I went out onto our porch every night to see if we could spot lights in the Benton windows. It wasn't until the end of the week that we saw one.

"They're here, Whit," I said.

"We'll go over tomorrow night to all the cottages," he told me.

And so we did. The next night, just before dark, Whitney, Clarrie, Cameron, and I went from door to door. We felt braver when there were four of us. We went to the back doors, of course; people always went to back doors if they wanted to sell something and if they lived on the peninsula all year.

I kept thinking about the Nickel-Plated Beauty. It gave me courage. But I don't know why I worried. Everybody wanted to buy berries and clams. They'd pay us a dime for a basket of wild strawberries and a nickel for a basket of the bigger berries. They'd also give us a dime for a full bucket of clams.

We saved the Benton cottage for last.

Mrs. Benton was always good to us. But she didn't open the door. Bessie Wilcox did. Bessie lived all year in Astoria, where she went to high school, but she came back to the peninsula every summer to live with her folks in Oysterville.

"Hello, Bessie," said Whit. "What are you doing here?"

Bessie was fairly nice, and we all liked her. "I'm working here this summer," she said, patting her head. She had a new hairstyle with bangs and lots of little falling curls. The bangs weren't real. They had a lot of blond in them and didn't match her brown hair.

Bessie filled the doorway, so we couldn't come in the way we used to. Cameron peeked around her. "Where's Mrs. Benton?"

Bessie had put on airs since we saw her last. "The Bentons went to Europe this summer—to Paris, France," she told us. "They let somebody else have the house."

"Who?" I asked.

"Mr. Amory. He's from Portland."

Just then a tall lady in a white dress came into the kitchen with a tray in her hands. She looked at us as if we weren't there, and spoke to Bessie. Her voice was sharp. "Is Philip's dinner ready yet, Bessie?"

"No, Ma'am, not quite," Bessie said. "You better taste the soup. I never made that kind before—not with cream."

Bessie had closed the screen door, but she hadn't got rid of us. "Ma'am, Mrs. Amory," I called out to the lady in white, "we came to ask you something. The Bentons used to buy raspberries and clams from us every summer. Would you be wanting to buy them, too?"

The lady smiled at us now. I still wasn't sure, though, if she really saw us. "Why, I suppose so. That would be very nice. Clam broth is nourishing." She picked up a spoon, tasted the soup, nodded, and left the kitchen. I could tell by the way her dress rustled that the starch in it could hold it up all by itself.

"That wasn't Mrs. Amory, Hester. Mrs. Amory went to Mount Hood. She hates the beach. That was Miss Lewis. She's the trained nurse." Bessie was mad. "You shouldn't have talked to her. Miss Lewis might not have liked it."

"Somebody sick here?" Clarrie asked.

Bessie shook her head. She shooed us away with her hands. "I have to get Philip's supper. You heard Miss Lewis. You'll have to go home now."

We walked past the house, but looked back once when we were in the middle of the road. Bessie had sure acted funny. It was close to dark now, but as we looked at the Benton house, we saw something. At an upstairs window one of the lace curtains was twitched back, and we saw a white face. It was a boy, with large dark eyes and whitish hair. He didn't smile. He only stared at us for a long, long time, and then, as we stared back, we saw Miss Lewis behind him. We saw her white arm reach out over him and close the curtains.

Cameron said, "I wonder who that was."

"I don't know," said Clarrie. "But whoever it was, that nurse lady didn't want him to look at us."

"Didn't know we were that bad," Whit spoke up. "Looked sort of like a ghost, didn't he?"

We walked home quietly as it got dark. I could smell the wild roses in bloom along the road. I don't know why, but I felt sad. Lots of summer folks would buy things from us. They'd been nicer so far this year than they'd ever been before. The redheaded

Addison girl had been in bed with a case of sunburn, so we hadn't even had to see her. I should have been happy. The twenty-seven dollars was getting closer all the time.

But somehow I couldn't forget the face of the boy at the window of the Benton house. He'd looked as if he wanted to ask us Kimballs something.

CHAPTER 4

Judge Amory

Now that everything was settled we went to bed early—not that we liked doing that—so we could get an early start in the morning. There was going to be a good low tide at five o'clock, and we meant to be on the beach, all except little Sarah, with our clam shovels and buckets. Later in the day I'd have to tell Aunt Rose I'd go to work for her. I hoped she wouldn't want me to start right off.

Just after sunrise Whitney woke up and roused the rest of us. We didn't get much of a breakfast—we'd come back for that later—but we each stuffed a hunk of bread and a piece of cheese in our overall pockets.

It was hard going, walking in the sand. The beach was a half mile away from our house, and we couldn't see it from the high dunes. Our beach was a long, long one. It stretched north and south just as far as we could see. There wasn't a rock or a headland on it. Miss Pitchford told us once that the atlases said it was the longest beach in the country. We'd always thought so, anyhow.

The waves were quiet this morning, and the ocean was a dark blue. The sky was so pale it was almost the color of skim milk. A little film of water lay over the sand, and it was fun to see our shadows in it. They were black and shiny. We'd left our shoes at home, and we began to run when we got onto the wet sand. We always did that, kicking the sand and water up behind us.

Jerry stayed behind to bark at some sand fleas in a big tangle of kelp. I guess they hopped on his nose and tickled him, but they didn't bite like dog fleas. Red went out to the waterline with us and dashed right into the surf. He bit a wave, howled, and jumped back. Red never could learn that the salt water hurt when it got up his nose.

"You get out of there, Red!" Whit yelled.

Cameron threw a driftwood stick and, with a wild yap, Red ran to fetch it. There wasn't much drifted stuff on the beach today. The weather had been too good for that, but sometimes the beach had lots of things on it, particularly when ships had foundered on the sandbars of Peacock Spit at the mouth of the Columbia River to the south. We'd found crates of red oranges— blood oranges—from Japan, logs that had come loose from logjams, round blue-green glass floats from fishing nets, and lots of other things. When there'd been a shipwreck, though, we couldn't go to the beach. That was when the men of the peninsula went out looking, because sometimes dead men were washed ashore.

Whit looked down at the sand. "Lots of clams here," he said, pointing to some little holes that looked as if somebody had made them with a sharp stick. He got the shovel ready. "I'll dig, Hester. You grab. We're the biggest. It's up to us to get three buckets to the one the others'll get."

That was all right with me. "But let me step on the holes first, Whit," I said.

Whit looked disgusted. "It'll take longer that way, and you know it doesn't always work. But go ahead."

I stepped on a hole. It squirted just fine, and Whit dug as fast as he could after the clam. "Now, Hester!" he yelled, pulling the shovel out.

I dived for the clam hole, stuck my hand

and part of my arm in up to my elbow, and hauled out a big yellowish razor clam. It was a beauty. "See, it does too work!" I told him. When there was a worm in the hole, it didn't squirt most of the time. I'd only stick my hand in where there were squirts, because I hated worms.

Clarrie and Tom, Cameron and Anna were digging, too, so we got our buckets full fast. The morning was good for clamming. Whit and I waded out and filled the buckets with ocean water before we left. The clams would keep fresh in salt water. We watched them stick their long bluish-white necks out when the buckets filled with water.

It was hard work lugging the splashy, heavy clam buckets back over the sand, even when we walked on the planks somebody had put down years back. At seven o'clock we got to the first house, the Petersons'. They took a half bucket and paid us. After that the clams sold everywhere we went, and wherever we went, I told them, "We'll bring some berries later on and some clams day after tomorrow, maybe. But we might bring crabs or fish instead."

Three of our clam buckets were empty when we finally got to the Bentons, and only about eighteen clams were in the bottom of the fourth bucket. Bessie came to the door again. "My, you're early," she said. "Miss Lewis isn't up yet." She took our bucket and emptied it into one on the floor of the back porch.

"Who's the boy we saw yesterday?" Cameron asked.

Bessie put her fingers to her lips. "That's Philip Amory. I think he's still asleep, poor little feller. He hasn't used his bell yet to call me."

"What bell? Why's he 'a poor little feller'?" Clarrie wanted to know.

"He's an invalid. When he wants something, he has a bell beside his bed to ring. He's been sick. Miss Lewis told me that he had infantile paralysis," Bessie explained.

"Can't he walk at all?" asked Anna.

Bessie shook her head. She hadn't pinned her false bangs on yet this early; she looked better. "No, he's in a wheelchair part of the time. They have to carry him around. His pa's up now, so you better get away from here. Mr. Amory's a very important man. He's a judge in Portland."

We were impressed. Judges sent bad people to jail. I took our money and we left. Once more we turned around to look up at the bedroom windows. Once more the same curtain was pulled back, and we saw the boy again. He looked at us and waved. We all waved back.

"Poor little feller," Clarrie said loudly, as we headed for home. "I'll bet he's still in bed from last night. Wouldn't it be awful to have to go to bed that early? It wasn't even dark when we saw him last night."

"I think I'll go see him," Cameron said.

I didn't like that at all. Cameron was mule-headed when he made up his mind. Mr. Amory was a judge. None of the other summer people had ever been that high and mighty before. I didn't think Judge Amory would want his son to be friends with the likes of us Kimballs, even if Mama had taught us good manners. I'd heard the summer folks call us "natives" and once, even, "the aborigines." Mrs. Johnson was a real native. She was half Indian. But we had nicer manners than to call her "native" to her face. The summer folks could be mean sometimes. Some of them looked down on us. This summer we couldn't afford to get mad at them. We had to keep on their good side if we were going to make enough to buy the Nickel-Plated Beauty.

We didn't have a single clam left over for

supper. We did have twenty cents to give Mama. That was what we usually earned in the summer when we went clamming, so we still had our secret twenty cents to put on the price of the stove.

All in all, we had thirty-five cents already—twenty from our clams and fifteen from chasing Bert Hogan's cows into his barn. Whitney took it out of his overall pocket and gave it to me before we went inside.

"What'll I do with it, Whit?" I asked him.

"You better hide it. Mama knows we haven't got any money. If she finds any around in the dresser drawers, she'll start asking questions."

"Where'll we hide it?"

"I don't know."

"I do," Clarrie spoke up. "There's a place in the barn."

We gave Mama her twenty cents, rinsed the buckets and shovels and put them in the sun to dry so they wouldn't rust, and then headed all in a bunch to the barn. Sarah was up by now, too. She tagged along with us.

"I saw Ginty nearly stick a hoof into this hole," Clarrie told us, pointing to a place in the barn floor near the cow stalls. "I filled it up again with dirt and put a board over it."

It was a good hiding place, all right. The board wasn't heavy at all. Even Sarah could lift it if she had to. Underneath the board the dirt was soft. I put the thirty-five cents in a blue bandanna, and as everybody watched I put it in the hole and covered it with the board.

Red and Jerry stood looking, too. Dogs can't talk, so it was all right with us if they knew where we hid our money.

After I ate my breakfast I got into my yellow dress, combed the snarls out of my hair and pinned it up with some of Mama's shell hairpins, washed my face and feet, and put on my shoes and stockings. Last of all I put on my best sunbonnet, the white muslin one. I don't know why I did all that just for Aunt Rose, who didn't care what I looked like as long as I was big enough to do lots of work. I felt like Sidney Carton, the man in *A Tale of Two Cities*, just before he walked up the steps to have his head chopped off by the guillotine during the French Revolution.

All of the other kids, little Sarah, too, were waiting on the porch when I came out. They had lard-pail berry buckets. Whit had also changed his clothes. He and I would walk to Nahcotta together. He'd go to the general store, and I'd go to the Palace Hotel.

Clarrie stepped up and shook my hand. Then Cameron, Anna, Tom, and Sarah shook it, too. Mama came out on the porch, a dish towel in one hand and a plate in the other. "Good luck, Hester," she said. "You don't have to stick it out all summer if it gets too bad, you know."

I nodded. I knew that, but I heard what Whit muttered to me. "You got to stick it out, Hester. You got to!"

All of us left at once. The other kids struck out north toward Oysterville. Whit and I went east to Nahcotta. I thought of a sentence from a book I'd borrowed from Miss Pitchford. "We march to our separate dooms," I told my brother.

"Oh, dry up," he said. "Summer won't last forever. I won't have to work for Mr. Willard till I'm an old man. It'll only seem that way. I'll go away to Ilwaco to high school pretty soon, and Mr. Willard'll have to get himself a new boy. Maybe Cameron will get stuck with the job next."

"I might have to work for Aunt Rose every summer of my life," I said. It was an awful thing to think.

Whit shook his head. He needed a haircut

again. "That'd be awful, Hester. I tell you what you ought to do. Drop some of Aunt Rose's dinner plates, and she'll get rid of you quick."

"I'll keep it in mind," I told him. "I might have to do something desperate."

I saw Aunt Rose's boarders, mostly old men with whiskers and old ladies with parasols, sitting on the front porch in rocking chairs. I looked for Dr. Alfred Perkins, who lived at the Palace Hotel all year round, but I didn't see him. He had come by our house a couple of days back with some syrupy tonic for Mama, who said she was feeling poorly. Dr. Alf looked a little like his brother Cedric, but he was bigger and wider. We liked Uncle Alfred. He wasn't really our uncle, of course, not even by marriage, but we were proud of him, because he never took anything off Aunt Rose—not even living there under the same roof.

Pa said Uncle Alf stood it, because he could drink Aunt Rose's coffee even better than she could and never once got heartburn from it. He even smoked cigars with her watching him. When anybody else smoked a pipe or cigar, she coughed and batted at the air until he put it away, but not Uncle Alfred. Uncle Ced smoked, too, but on the sly. He kept his pipe in the woodshed and his tobacco in the barn, so she'd never find them both together and throw them out.

The doctor never married. Nobody knew why. If there was a sad story about him, we never heard it. I even asked him about it once while Mama tried to hush me up. "Married?" he said. "No, Hester, not me. I've always been too busy. Maybe if you people here on the peninsula could refrain from getting sick so much, I'd have time to cast my eye around for a good-looking widow with lots of money." He'd looked hard at me, grinning. "Why do you ask, Hester? Are you proposing to me?"

I got red in the face then. "I was thinking of Miss Pitchford."

Uncle Alf pretended to shiver. "I never did have an eye for yellow-haired women, Hester, and schoolmarms still scare me after twenty-five years of being out of school."

We all laughed at this, but I was disappointed. I liked matchmaking, even if Pa did call it the most dangerous game in the world.

As I got closer to the Palace Hotel, I decided that Dr. Alf must be out on a call and turned to the back door. If I was to work for Aunt Rose, that's what I'd have to use.

She wasn't very proud of us Kimballs and thought her sister had married beneath her.

Aunt Rose was shaking out a mop when she spotted me coming up the back steps. "What brings you here, Hester? Your mother still sick?" she asked, dust from her mop filling the air above me until I sneezed.

"Ka-choo!" I said, and then I sneezed again. "No, Mama's just fine. I came on my own, Aunt Rose. If you still want me to work for you, I'll come."

She hauled the mop in and leaned on it. I'd given her a surprise. "Well, will wonders never cease? Do your pa and ma know about this?"

"Sure. They said I was to keep the tips. You and Mama both said that."

"That's right, Hester." Her eyes, like blue-agate marbles, got squinty and narrow. "How come you decided all of a sudden to help your Aunt Rose out?"

I told her what I'd told Mama, about the dress in the wish book. I knew already that if you sounded grabby and greedy enough about yourself, nearly everybody would believe you. She believed me.

Aunt Rose nodded. "Vanity, eh? Well, that's just about what I thought. The railroad men haven't come along yet to measure your pa's wood, have they? He could have worked for me, but he wanted to be his own boss. See what it got him? His kids go out working for other people. I suppose you want that dress so you can go to the square dances at Ilwaco and catch yourself a beau. Got your hair up, too, haven't you?"

I didn't have anything to say to this, mean though it was. It was just Aunt Rose's way of talking to people. And what could Pa do around there in the winters? There wasn't enough work for Uncle Cedric to do. Aunt Rose told Mama that she wished she could hire him out to somebody, but there wasn't a crying thing he could do but walk out and pick up oysters on the Nahcotta flats at low tide. Nobody in Nahcotta bought oysters, when any child five years old could stroll out after them, so Aunt Rose and Uncle Cedric had a hard time making ends meet in the winter, too. She was just talking big.

"Rosie, Rosie!" I heard a call, and Uncle Ced stuck his head out of the back door. "There's somebody new just come in. He's at the desk wanting a room."

"I'll be there directly, Ced," she shouted. She turned to me. "I've got no more time to waste now, Hester. Ced and I can get the breakfasts, but you be here at eight-thirty tomorrow morning. You'll be paid twenty-five cents a day, and you can have your tips. I keep my promises. Do you want to stay here nights? We've got a spare room up under the eaves that's too little to rent out."

I backed off. "No, Ma'am, I'll stay home nights. When do I get off work?"

"At six o'clock, after you've waited on tables at supper. Ced does the dishes every night. We can't have you walking home after dark, and we won't have the time to take you. Our paying guests need a lot of looking after, I can tell you."

In a flash she was gone. You could almost feel the breeze her black skirts made. I don't know why Aunt Rose always wore black. She wasn't in mourning for anyone I knew about.

Uncle Cedric held the screen door open for her. He looked at me and winked. "I heard what Rose said, Hester. It'll be nice having you around here this summer." He was wearing an apron, a green-and-white one, and he didn't even take it off when I kept looking at it.

As I started back to Ocean Park, I wasn't as all-fired sure that it would be nice being around the Palace Hotel all summer as Uncle Ced was. I thought of going into the general store to tell Whit it was settled and try to peek at the Nickel-Plated Beauty to get my spirits up past my shoe tops. But I didn't. I didn't want to have to look at Mr. Willard again.

I didn't hurry home. I wandered by the Benton house. Some people were sitting on the front porch. I could tell Miss Lewis right off by her white uniform, and the sick boy by the strange chair with big wheels he was sitting in. A man in a straw hat and a long whitish-yellow coat sat in a Boston rocker. Bessie came out the front door with a big white-and-red cookie jar as I watched. When I got closer I could see who the others were, and I let out a gasp. My brothers, Cameron and Tom, and my sisters, Clarrie, Anna, and Sarah, were sitting on the steps eating. The dogs lay panting in the sand in front of the house. Our berry buckets sat in a shiny row on the lowest step. What in thunder were they doing with the Amorys? I asked myself.

Cameron got up and ran to me, nearly knocking over a bucket. "Hester," he yelled, "you come tell the judge about me."

I wanted to shake him. "What have you gone and done, Cameron? You stay away from that judge."

"He's nice. We like him. He bought fifteen cents' worth of wild strawberries from us. I asked about Philip, and he carried him downstairs to the front porch, so he could meet us. Philip had asked him all about us already."

"What does the judge want to know about you?"

"He wants to know about my references."

"What are references?"

"I don't know, Hester. I asked him if we could take Philip out on the beach to play with us, and he laughed and said we'd have to have references. I told him you were my big sister and you'd know all about my references."

I thought hard. Cameron's mouth had cookie crumbs at the corners. Judge Amory must be all right if he fed us Kimballs. I went with my brother to the porch, glad I had on my yellow dress and my good sunbonnet. The Amorys could see from looking at me, dressed up the way I was, that we were mannered people, even if we were "natives."

Judge Amory stood up when I got to the top step. I nodded, but I felt like curtsying the way the ladies did all the time in *The Three Musketeers*. He was tall and thin and pale-haired, too, and had a nice smile, with lots of gold teeth showing in it. "Miss Kimball—Hester Kimball?" He was very polite.

I said, "Yes, sir." Then I asked, "You wanted to know about my brother Cameron?"

The judge had a very deep voice for a skinny man. "Your brother says he'll take Philip to the beach each warm, sunny afternoon for an hour if we pay him twenty-five cents a week. Quite an enterprising family, aren't you? What are you going to do with all this money you're making?"

It wouldn't do to lie to a judge. "It's a secret, sir, but it's honest." I took a sugar cookie from the jar when Bessie offered it. The judge took one, too.

"I'm sure it is. Well, if you say your brother is trustworthy and you can figure some way to get Philip there in a wheelchair, I'm game for it. Philip wants to go."

I looked at Philip Amory. His dark eyes, as soft a brown as Jerry's, were on my face. His feet and legs were covered by a blanket. I could tell just by looking at him that Philip wanted to go.

"Cameron, how are you going to do it?"
I asked my brother. I knew him. If he'd
asked the judge, he'd already figured it out.

"We'll go on the old planks. They're only
a little way from here, and one of them is
just wide enough for the wheels. The hardest thing will be to get the wheelchair off
the porch."

"I don't think that will be too difficult,"
said Miss Lewis. "Why don't you do what
they do in hospitals? Build a ramp at the
side of the steps. They're plenty wide. I saw
some planks in the woodshed this morning
that would do just fine."

The judged smiled. "That's a capital idea,
Miss Lewis. I'll make the ramp for Philip
myself. The exercise will do me good." He
looked at us six Kimballs. "Fine-looking
family," he said. "Your parents must be
proud of such strapping, healthy young-
sters." His voice was loud, but his eyes were
as sad as Philip's.

"Thank you. I'll tell Mama what you
said," I told him. Judge Amory really wasn't
scary, for all he was such a great man.
"Cameron will take real good care of your
boy."

"I have no doubt of it," said Judge
Amory. He spoke now to my brother. "You

be here at two P.M. sharp every day but Sunday, Cameron. Bessie or Miss Lewis will help you take Philip down the ramp. Yes, I think it would do him good to get out in the fresh air again. That's why we came here. Philip used to be quite an athlete." The judge patted his chest. "Just sniff that sea air. It'll put roses in your cheeks, Philip."

"Yes, Papa." I heard Philip's voice for the first time. It was low and soft.

Soon after that we left the Amorys, and I went along with the others as they sold the last of their wild strawberries to the Wagners and the Masons. Cameron fished the money out and gave it to me. It was another twenty-five cents. We'd made nearly half a dollar that day and, with the cow-chasing money, we had sixty cents. Mama knew about the berry picking. She had to know it when we took all the lard pails off the back porch. Nobody asked me how it had gone with Aunt Rose, and I was just as glad. I didn't want to talk about her.

As we walked home, Vestal and Virgil Johnson came out of a big Scotch-broom bush at the bend of the road. They had lard pails with them, too. The Johnsons were shorter than we were. They had shiny blue-black hair and snub noses like their ma, and strange greenish eyes like their pa.

"We went to your house to play," Vestal said to Clarrie, who was her age. "Your ma said you went berrying, so we got buckets, too, and came along to find you."

Virgil, her brother, who was only a month older than Cameron, put in with, "We hear tell you're going to work at the Palace Hotel, Hester. I bet you'll be earning lots of money."

I knew Mama had probably told them, but before I could say anything, Tom piped up. I wished I could have hushed him, but it was too late. "We are. We're digging clams and crabbing and picking berries to earn money to buy something with."

"Tommy Kimball!" I cried. "You tattled!"

"I didn't neither. I never told them it was a stove we wanted to buy for Mama," he said, facing me.

The secret was out now. The Johnsons knew. They weren't tattletales. If we asked them to keep our secret, they would, and nobody could pry it out of them. But they were the biggest copycats on the peninsula. They copied everything we did.

Virgil looked at Vestal. "Ma could use a

new stove," he said. "Guess we could try to make some money, too. Mind if we go along with you?"

"Yes, I mind. You can sell your berries and clams in Nahcotta," I said, as fierce as I could. "We got all the summer people signed up here already. They won't pay you any more than they pay us, so you keep away from them. Won't do you no good to try."

They weren't mad at all. They never got mad, it seemed to me, even when I saw bright red. Mama said it was a real compliment, just about the best one of all, to be copied, but just the same I got sick and tired of it.

Vestal spoke up. "That's a good idea you gave us, Hester. There's lots more people at Nahcotta than at Ocean Park."

"Oh, let's go home," I told my brothers and sisters. But I yelled back at the Johnsons, "Don't you dare tattle on us Kimballs."

We had another surprise at home—and it had been a day just full of them—for we passed a strange man driving our chestnut horse, Regent. Pa had traded Regent with the stranger, a man from Ilwaco, for a dandy little black gelding named Henry Bender. There was just one thing wrong with

Henry Bender. He was in fine shape, but he got winded easily in the sea air. Pa had told the stranger that practically everybody felt that way for a while at the beach because of the low altitude, but after a time the salt air always braced them up. Henry Bender would be just fine once he got his sea legs.

CHAPTER 5

Aunt Rose's Palace Hotel

It was nice to think that we had three jobs now—Cameron's, mine at the Palace Hotel, and Whit's at the general store, although Whit didn't bring in anything that he could put on the stove. I thought it was good, though, that he was there to keep an eye on Mr. Willard. I still didn't trust him, even though he'd signed our paper and we'd signed his.

Cameron told Pa and Mama all about Philip Amory and how he was to take him out on the beach every day. He didn't say that he was getting paid for it. Mama might not have liked knowing that he took money for doing a good deed for someone who was sick.

We all went clamming the next morning and did nearly as well as the day before. We brought home fifteen cents to Mama, and had fifteen cents for ourselves. We told Mama a fib, but it wasn't much of one. She wondered why we kept taking four buckets, and I said it was because we kept hoping we could get all four filled up. I began to think I'd tell a lot of white lies before this was all over.

While the others did their morning chores before they went out berrying, I hurried with my own chore of fixing up the lamps. Because she knew I was going to start work for Aunt Rose that day, Mama didn't ask me to do the breakfast dishes. She did them while I put on my blue-calico print dress, and when I came downstairs again, she gave me her prettiest apron, with the pale-blue rickrack trim around the edges and on the pocket. I felt like crying, but I only said, "Thanks, Mama."

Pa was going to cut wood south of Nahcotta today, so he gave Whit and me a ride in the wagon behind Maude and Prince. I liked to ride behind the two big white workhorses, the best skidding team for logs on the peninsula, everybody said. They moved slowly and carefully, their big hooves sinking deep into the sand. I was proud to be seen with them.

When we went by the old Benton place, I stood up in the wagon to get a good look. Judge Amory had been as good as his word. He'd gone to the Benton's woodshed and built a ramp for Philip's wheelchair. It would be easy as pie for Cameron to get Philip to the beach now.

When we reached Nahcotta, Pa called out, "Whit, we're here. You help your sister down."

"Aw, she can get down by herself," Whit said.

Pa looked fierce. "Not in that dress she can't. She might tear it, and she's got to look fine to work at the hotel."

Whit growled, but he jumped down and held up his hands. I didn't want to be helped any more than he wanted to do it, but I let him. Pa took notions sometimes. This was one of the times.

"Whit," Pa went on, "I have to have a bottle of horse liniment and a bottle of Cox's Horse Tonic. Henry Bender's off his feed."

Whit didn't know what to say. His ears got reddish. He didn't want to have to ask Mr. Willard to put anything else on our bill. "Pa!" he said, and he made it sound unhappy.

Pa knew what he meant right off. He

reached into the pocket of his vest, not the one he kept his tobacco plug in, but the one under his old silver-plated watch. He got out a fifty-cent piece, looked at it, sighed, and flipped it to Whit, who caught it in the air. "That'll cover it," he said. "Maybe there'll be a penny or two over. Get a peppermint or a licorice stick apiece for you and your sister after you get off work. Just don't tell your brothers and sisters. It's all I can spare."

Whitney grinned. He patted his lunch pail. "Thanks, Pa, but I'll have mine after my lunch. I'll save a peppermint for Hester."

"By, Whit," I said. "Wish me good luck."

"Best of luck," Whit said, and then he whistled. "That's Mr. Willard on the porch. He's got his watch out. I'm late!" And in a flash Whit was gone.

I was all alone. I walked slowly to my doom. I thought of another sentence from Miss Pitchford's books. "Hell yawns for the evil man." Aunt Rose's back door yawned for me, but I hadn't done anything bad enough to deserve it.

Holding my breath, I went into the kitchen. There wasn't anybody around at all, but there was a big heap of dirty dishes piled up on the drainboards next to the sink and the pump. I stood looking around, wondering what I was supposed to do. The coffeepot was boiling away on one of the kitchen stoves, and something else was cooking in the biggest white pot I ever saw. The steam coming from it smelled delicious. Except for her coffee, Aunt Rose was a good cook. I was pretty sure from the smell that it was going to be chicken. I hoped for dumplings, too. Aunt Rose hadn't told me to bring my lunch, so I thought maybe she was going to feed me at noon. Chicken and dumplings were a favorite of mine.

While I was standing there sniffing the smells, the kitchen door swung open and Aunt Rose came through it with Uncle Ced behind her. Uncle Ced had his hands full. He was carrying a big round tray, stacked high with cups and saucers. Aunt Rose carried a big coffeepot. Looking like a thundercloud, she slammed the coffeepot down on the long kitchen worktable.

"Well, of all the gall!" she said. "To want to drink tea in the morning, of all things! I never heard of such an idea, and in Washington Territory, too. You'd think we were in London, England. It's outlandish, Ced."

Uncle Cedric was mild as always. "Now, Rosie, if you'd put some water in your coffee, it'd be just dandy. They don't like it. You've got to please the folks if you want them to come here to the hotel."

Aunt Rose saw me. "Hester," she snapped, "don't just stand there. Get to work. Ced'll tell you what to do until I get back." She was gone again, her last words floating to me from the back porch. I unfolded Mama's apron and put it on.

Uncle Ced set the tray down carefully. He smiled at me. "Good morning, Hester. I guess the first order of the day is to do the breakfast dishes. Rosie's pretty particular. I'll show you how she wants them done."

He did show me, too. She had her own way of washing, rinsing, and drying. When he thought I had the hang of it, he went off, saying that he had to fix up the gentlemen's chambers while Aunt Rose fixed up the ladies'. They were short a girl to work upstairs.

Aunt Rose popped in and out a lot that morning. Once I'd finished the dishes to suit her, there were other things to do—polish the silver, scrub the floor, fix the vegetables for lunch, all sorts of things. She kept at me every minute.

When I was done with shelling the peas for lunch, I went out on the back porch. Uncle Ced was scrubbing out the brass cuspidors. I was sure glad I didn't have to do that chore. I didn't like tobacco chewing any more than the other women on the peninsula, but the men liked it and they kept on doing it, even when they had to empty their own spittoons the way Pa did. "The day will come," Mama often said to Clarrie and Anna and me, "when the women of the United States and all the territories will rise up and prevail, and the cuspidor will be a thing of the past." We were still waiting, though.

"What'll I do now, Uncle Ced?" I asked him. As far as I could see, the kitchen was all ready for lunch.

"You just wait," he said. "She'll be along pretty soon. She'll find something for you to do, don't worry, Hester." He seemed almost to admire his wife. "Rosie should have been a general," he said.

I waited, and pretty soon along came Aunt Rose with a feather duster in her hand. I saw her from outside the screen and shot back into the kitchen fast.

"Been keeping Ced from his chores?" she asked me.

I shook my head. "No, Ma'am. I just wanted to know what he had in mind for me to do next."

She jabbed a long fork into the big pot on the fire and nodded. "Ced ain't got no mind, Hester, not any that counts, anyways. The chicken's done. Good. You pull out the bay leaves. I put three bay leaves in it. Be sure you get them all."

I got a big spoon from the clean dishes and waited while she dragged the big pot over on the back of the stove to simmer. Aunt Rose was real strong.

Then she put down her fork and looked at me. "Just one thing we have to get straight here, Hester. You ask *me* about the work, do you hear? I give Ced the orders. You don't ask him unless I tell you to. He doesn't know anything."

"Yes, Ma'am," I said. I knew he could hear every word she said because of the wide-open window. If I'd been Uncle Ced, I'd have thrown a cuspidor through the window right there and then.

I was scared when I hauled out the bay leaves, but I didn't spill anything, even when Aunt Rose glared at me. Then she showed me how to set the table. She was sure fancy. She had a red doily under every plate and a silver-plated caster in the center. She didn't use oilcloth, either, the way we did. She had white linen cloths, so white they hurt your eyes to look at them.

I hung around the stove while she made the dumplings, dropping great gobs of the sticky dough into the chicken pot and slamming the lid down tight to steam them. They soon rose right up, tilted the lid, and made it rattle. I wanted to grin when she made another pot of coffee and put lots of water in it, but I didn't dare. It wasn't often anybody licked Aunt Rose.

Uncle Ced came in now to wash his hands under the pump. He'd done his outside chores, splitting the kindling wood and feeding the team that brought the guests from the ferryboat landing where the *Harvest Queen* dumped them off. He didn't look at me at all. "Is it time yet, Rose?" he asked.

"Five minutes to noon, Cedric," said Aunt Rose. She had a little watch pinned to the front of her dress, and she peeked under the bib of her apron to see it. "We're real punctual around here, Hester, you'll see. You were five minutes late this morning. I saw you out the window. You'll make it up tonight by leaving five minutes after six, won't you?"

"Yes, Ma'am," I said.

"We'll eat later, the three of us," she told me. Then she called out, "Time, Ced!"

Uncle Cedric picked up a handbell from a kitchen shelf and went out the door. I listened while he rang it, and then Aunt Rose and I began to take the big dishes of food into the dining room. I had to be careful how I walked, some people came in so fast. Others were leaning on canes. Most of them were old people, the old people I'd seen on the front porch.

Everybody dug into the chicken and everything else. Aunt Rose stood at the door, her arms folded. She was a different Rose now. She even smiled at her guests as they ate, and laughed at the old men's jokes, but when she looked at me and pointed toward the plates, her eyes snapped the same old way.

I got a tray and stacked six plates on it, and the dirty silverware, too. Then I came back twice more. It was heavy work.

"Serve the coffee, Hester. Ced'll help you," she hissed, as I went by for the last time to the kitchen.

Uncle Ced had the cups and saucers, all sixteen of them, on a tray. I set each cup and saucer down the way I'd been taught.

Nobody took much notice of me except to nod. Some of the old ladies smiled a little bit, though. They smelled sweet, of Florida water and rice powder.

"My sister's child," I heard Aunt Rose say once to one of them, as I poured the coffee, praying that I wouldn't get it down somebody's back. Some of the old men were deaf, and they didn't hear "Excuse me" very well.

I got things done all right, I guess, because Aunt Rose didn't have anything to say to me. I turned around once to ask her something, but she was gone. I waited again, and in a minute she was back with bowls of shortcake, dripping with strawberries and with mountains of whipped cream on top.

"Strawberries! Land sakes, real honest-to-goodness wild strawberries, aren't they, Mrs. Perkins?" said an old lady, who had gold hairpins half falling out of her hair.

"That they are," Aunt Rose agreed. I looked at the strawberries, and all at once I guessed where they had come from. My guess didn't make me happy one bit.

The guests and the travelers made short work of the shortcake. They folded their napkins and left to go to their rooms for a nap or to the porch. One of the commercial travelers left me a nickel tip. Nobody else left anything. We cleared off the tables and took away the dirty cloths. Some of the old folks were sure messy eaters, and I thought Aunt Rose should have used oilcloth.

The three of us ate in the kitchen. We had everything the guests had, but not as much and not as good. Where they had chicken drumsticks and breasts and whole dumplings, we had wings and necks and pieces of dumplings and potatoes that had broken apart while boiling. Only the peas were the same.

Although there wasn't any shortcake left, I couldn't get my mind off the wild strawberries. I finally got up the grit to ask, "Where'd the wild strawberries come from, Aunt Rose?"

"From the Johnson children." That was exactly what I had suspected. "They came here real early this morning. I was just setting the fires in the stoves." She took a sip of coffee from the first coffeepot. "Now they are what I'd call enterprising children—not like some I could mention, who don't think of anything but what they can put on their backs. I was glad to see those berries. I hadn't a single idea of what to have for lunch except bread pudding, and we had that yesterday. They said they'd bring clams, too, if I wanted them. I asked them what they were going to do with all of the money they'll be making, and you'll never guess what they told me."

"They're buying something for their mother," I said. I put my fork down with a clatter that made Uncle Cedric jump.

Aunt Rose's mouth fell open. Then she closed it with a snap. "Well, they must have told you, too. Half of Nahcotta's buying from them. Why didn't you Kimballs think of that? Your ma could use plenty of things—particularly now, I suppose."

"We know," I told her, and I got up and started the dishes without being told to.

All afternoon it was, "Hester, clean this pot. I need it." "Hurry up, Hester, do that dusting in the guests' parlor right now." "Haven't you finished peeling the potatoes yet?" "Don't you know how to do anything right? Here, let me show you." She kept Uncle Ced and me hopping. We didn't have any time to talk at all, and she never said, "Thank you," or "That's a good job, Hester." And I knew I did good work.

I didn't care much about that, though. I was mad at myself for giving Vestal and Virgil the idea to come to Nahcotta. Why hadn't I thought of bringing berries and clams to Aunt Rose? I came here every morning anyhow. Now I considered asking Aunt Rose to buy them from us, but thought better of it. She'd only say I should have had the idea first. Besides, I knew it wouldn't be fair. The Johnsons got to her before we did.

Dinner was served at five o'clock. I washed the dirty pots and pans that were empty and that I could lift, and I watched the clock, too. At five forty-five I helped bring in the dirty plates, and at five after six I took off Mama's apron.

Aunt Rose looked at the kitchen clock, checked it with her watch, and said, "It's five minutes fast, Hester."

"What is?" I asked.

"The clock."

I scoured another pot, and then when she looked at her watch and said it was time for me to go, I went.

"Good night, Hester," Uncle Ced called out. He was already finishing the dishes.

"Don't be late again tomorrow," said Aunt Rose.

It was pretty outside. The air smelled fresh and clean. It had rained in the afternoon, but now that it was close to sunset, the sky was streaky with pink, orange, and yellow clouds. In between, the sky was dark blue. Tomorrow was going to be nice. Much good that would do me, shut up in the kitchen of the Palace Hotel.

Whit was waiting for me, sitting on the steps of the general store. "How'd it go, Hester?" he asked, jumping down. He had the liniment and the tonic for Henry Bender stuffed in his pockets, and they gurgled as he handed me my peppermint. It had fuzz on it from being in his pocket and tasted funny, but I sucked it just the same.

"About what we expected, Whit. Aunt Rose sure knows how to get her money's worth out of a hired girl. Uncle Ced was right."

"What'd he say?"

" 'Rose should have been a general.' "

Whit laughed as we started home. "Just like Mr. Willard. What else happened?"

I told him about the Johnsons and how "enterprising" they were. Whit wasn't happy about it, either.

"Didn't waste time, did they?"

"Not a doggone minute."

"Well, buck up. I have an idea that'll make us more cash. It'll make you feel better."

"What is it?"

"It's about the Fourth of July picnic in Ilwaco. You know all the races they have every year, the footraces and the gunnysack races and the potato races?"

"What about them?"

"I heard a man in the store say that they'll be giving out money instead of ice cream for prizes this year."

I wanted to sit down when I heard that. My feet hurt all at once. That was what came of wearing my best high-top shoes with tassels. I'd know better tomorrow.

"We'll get in training. We've got two weeks yet. We're going to enter every race we can. We're bound to win a couple."

"You'd better not count on me, Whit," I said. "I'm going to be too tired. I think I'd better get in training just to keep up with Aunt Rose."

"Cameron and Tom and I will have to do it then," he said. "Running races is man's work."

"Wait till you tell that to Clarrie," I said. Clarrie was the fastest girl runner I ever saw.

I didn't say very much more as we walked home. I couldn't stop thinking about those Johnsons. They'd probably get every berry and clam on the peninsula before the Fourth of July came.

CHAPTER 6

The Not-So-Glorious Fourth

I told the others what Aunt Rose had said about Vestal and Virgil. They got as mad as I did, but then Whit pointed out that there were seven of us to go after things while there were only two Johnsons. That made me feel better, but just the same, it still rubbed me the wrong way that they had sewed up the Palace Hotel and my very own relations.

That night Pa went out into the barn and curried Henry Bender after supper, and we all went along to see him drench the horse and give him his tonic. Henry Bender still looked poorly. Pa showed Cameron how to rub liniment on him. Cameron liked horses a lot; he had a way with them, just like Pa.

I liked sitting in the barn on a bale of hay. It was good to be home, and I felt warm toward everyone. There was nothing like going out in the world to make you like your own family, even if the next minute you got mad at one of them. Prince and Maude stomped softly in their stalls. Jerry and Red came to flop at my feet in the hay. Willoughby, who hated the dogs, got on top of a stall to rub against my ear. Ginty and Jersey had been milked a long time ago. That was one of Clarrie's chores. She was the best milker in the family.

I yawned. "Better get to bed, Hester," Pa said, wiping the shivering Henry Bender down on one side with a soft cloth while Cameron wiped the other.

"How's Henry Bender, Pa?" I asked.

"Poorly, Hester. I think maybe his owner tuckered him out."

"You'll untucker him, Pa," Tom piped up.

It was way past Tom's bedtime, so I took his hand and we got up from the hay bale. Pa called out to me at the barn door. "How was Uncle Ced? Haven't seen him lately."

I shook my head. "I don't know, Pa. He leads a hard life."

Pa stopped working over Henry Bender for a minute. "Don't see how Ced stands it. Mark my words, one of these days Cedric Perkins is going to crack."

"He doesn't show any signs of it so far,"
I said. "Good night, Pa." There wasn't anything more to say, so I took Tom in the
house and put him to bed, even if he didn't
want to go. Late as it was, Mama was still
up, ironing a fresh apron for me to wear
tomorrow.

We went clamming again the next morning. It was the last low morning tide for
June, and we had to make the most of it. We
were on the beach as early as we could get
there, but we found the Johnsons had arrived even earlier. We all marched right up
to them and stood there before we dug a
single clam.

"Look here!" said Whit. "You quit copying us. You quit digging our clams."

Virgil reached down to grab for a clam.
He got it, a real big one, too. Vestal kept on
digging. "It ain't your beach," said Virgil.
"It doesn't belong to anybody, unless it be-
longs to Uncle Sam."

We knew the beach belonged to the
United States, all right; we didn't have to be
told that. But it stopped us for a minute. It
sort of stuck in our craws.

"Well, we'll split the beach up," Whit
went on. "You live north of us, so you take

the north half. That log on the beach can be our marker. We'll dig south of it."

Virgil shook his head. His black hair flopped over his eyes as bad as Whit's did. "No," he said, "that ain't fair, Whit Kimball. We live north like you said, but we sell our stuff in Nahcotta. We'd have to walk farther with the heavy buckets. You take the north."

Whit wasn't too happy about that, but he nodded. I wasn't through, though. "Same thing goes on the berry picking, then. We'll take the north. You take the south."

Vestal and Virgil nodded. It was fine with them, even if they didn't grin about it.

"See that you don't do any forgetting on purpose," Clarrie said fiercely to Vestal.

Cameron jerked his head toward the log. "You're north of that log already. Get going south right now, Virgil." The Johnsons took up their buckets and went. Cameron stood watching as they started to dig just south of the marker. "I don't think I'm ever going to trust those Johnsons again. Too doggone smart," he said to us, his hands on his hips.

"Oh, stop talking and start digging, Cameron," Whit ordered.

After we delivered our clams to the summer homes, we practiced for the Fourth of July races. Whit drew a line in the sand, and Clarrie, Cameron, Anna, and Tom, who were in training, each got down on one knee. When Whit yelled, "Go!" they all dashed off as fast as they could. I carried the four empty buckets.

"Hey, if you get home earlier than I do, you can do my chores, too," I yelled. I thought that would bring them up short or at least slow them down to a smart trot, but it didn't.

Then I put in another day at Aunt Rose's. It was a lot like the one before. I worked like a beaver, but at least Uncle Alf came into the kitchen and talked to Uncle Cedric and me while I cleaned the silver casters. He asked me how things went. I couldn't really tell him with Uncle Ced listening, so I just sighed and said, "Just fine, Uncle Alf."

Uncle Alf poured himself a cup of Aunt Rose's black coffee. He pretended to shake like a dog after he took the first sip. "Bitter brew," he said, making a terrible face that made me giggle. Dr. Alf was fun.

"What's infantile paralysis?" I asked him, while I wiped off the silverware.

"It's a bad disease, Hester, that cripples the muscles of one's arms and legs. Why do you want to know?"

"Because Philip Amory had it, and he's crippled."

"Who's Philip Amory?" he asked.

While I told him all about Philip and Judge Amory, Uncle Alf went on drinking his coffee. He sighed. "It's too bad about the boy, Hester. There's not much we can do about that disease."

Then Uncle Alf put his coffee cup down. He took out his gold watch, looked at it, and snapped it shut. I loved his watch. It played "The Blue Danube" waltz when he had it open.

"I have to go now, Hester. It was nice talking to you. I'll be getting out your way real soon to see your mother again."

"Is she sick?" I asked, getting scared.

"Nothing that time won't cure," he told me with a smile. Uncle Alf timed it just right going out of the kitchen, because as he left Aunt Rose came in the swinging door. "Morning, Rosie," he said.

"Good morning, Dr. Perkins," she told him. And then she started giving me orders again.

That was how it went for about ten days. Whit worked, I worked, and Cameron and the others picked berries and took Philip Amory out in his wheelchair every day.

I got paid on Saturday night. I took the money home to Mama, who was happy to get it. I also had forty cents in tips—thirty cents from commercial travelers and ten cents from one of the old men.

We went out for crabs now, looking in the tide pools. Crabbing was even more tricky than clamming. We had to chase the crabs around with nets to catch them, and when we finally got one out of the water, we often had to throw him back, because he was too little. When we looked down through six or seven feet of water to a sandy bottom, things seemed bigger than they really were.

Some days we didn't find any crabs at all. The days we didn't, the little kids would go to Nahcotta with worms and fish off the dock. The fish were so thick there that they could bait five hooks and pull out every one with a perch or a sunfish on it.

By the first of July we had six dollars—all in nickels, pennies, and dimes. We didn't dare change our money for silver dollars, and we didn't trust paper money at all. But any way we looked at it, the Nickel-Plated Beauty was getting closer to our kitchen.

All of us but me kept in training. We were in good shape by the time the Fourth of July came around. It didn't matter that I hadn't trained for the races, because I didn't have the Fourth off. A party from Astoria was coming up that day, and I had to help out at the hotel.

I got a ride again to the Palace Hotel in the wagon. Everyone else was dressed up for the picnic, and I got down at Nahcotta feeling sorry for myself that I wasn't going to Ilwaco with them. Our great-aunt, who lived there, would have a picnic lunch for them, probably ham, hot potato salad, and pickled eggs. I wondered what Aunt Rose would have. Whatever it was, it wouldn't make up for not hearing the brass band play all day. I was to stay at the hotel until the family came back from Ilwaco to get me. They'd be back after dark. Then I'd hear all about the picnic.

Aunt Rose was mad as a wet hen when I came in the back door. I didn't know why; I wasn't late. Her eyebrows were together as she did the breakfast dishes. "Hester, we're shorthanded today, and with those Astoria people coming, too! Uncle Ced's gone."

"Where'd he go?" I couldn't help asking. This was the first time he hadn't been there working.

She picked up a saucer and nearly broke it, banging it down so hard. "He took off for Ilwaco. That Dr. Alf Perkins put it into Cedric's head to go to the celebration. He wouldn't have thought of it by himself. He wouldn't dare."

I pulled my apron on over my head quick, so she wouldn't see me grin. So Uncle Ced got away! Was he beginning to crack? I was glad for him and would have liked to give him three cheers.

Aunt Rose didn't say any more about it then, and we sure worked hard. I knew pretty much what to do by now without asking and without her telling me, and she worked right alongside me, not having time to give me lots of orders. We fed the guests, all twenty-two of them, lunch and dinner. Aunt Rose kept muttering all day. As the hours went by, she got madder and madder.

I kept waiting to hear Whit at the back door. I wanted to be out of there when Aunt Rose's husband finally returned, but I didn't hear my brother. We waited and waited. I sat at the table while Aunt Rose drank coffee and walked around the kitchen muttering. All the work was done. It got to be nine-thirty, and still nobody came.

"Men!" Aunt Rose snapped out at me. "The trouble with the whole world is men, Hester! Who is it who goes to war all the time? It's men, that's who it is. Don't you ever forget what I tell you about men."

"Yes, Ma'am," I said, but what I really thought was that there were too many Aunt Roses around. A whole world of Aunt Roses would make men go to war just to get away from home and have a little peace and quiet. I like men—all except Mr. Willard. He ought to have married Aunt Rose.

And just then we heard it—the creak of the wagon and Pa's voice. They were here, coming around the side of the hotel. Pa favored the back door, too.

Pa was laughing. "Steady there, Ced," he called out. "Hold on to the wheel. Don't fall off."

"Ced!" Aunt Rose cried. She went to the screen.

I got up, watching the door. I heard footsteps on the stairs. They seemed to be dragging a little. Was Uncle Cedric hurt? Pa came into the kitchen, and Uncle Ced was with him. "That you, Rosie?" he said in a funny voice.

Aunt Rose had gone as white as one of her tablecloths. She just kept looking at him.

"Is he sick?" I asked her.

"No, Hester, he's drunk—he's as drunk as a hoot owl!"

Uncle Ced leaned against the drainboard. He had to catch hold of the pump handle to keep his balance, and water shot out all over the kitchen wall.

Aunt Rose woke up fast. "Look what you're doing to my house, Cedric Perkins. You get upstairs this minute and don't let any of my guests hear you, either. I've never been so ashamed in my life."

Uncle Ced pointed a finger at her. "Whose house, Rose? My house, too, isn't it? I'm getting sick and tired of you always taking credit for the hotel. I can't even smoke in my own house."

She gasped. "Where've you been all day?"

"The Last Chance Saloon in Ilwaco. That's where I've been." He grinned at her, showing all of his teeth.

Pa was upset. I could tell it by the way he edged toward the door. Uncle Ced swept out his arm and got him by the coat sleeve. "Don't go yet, Joe. I want a witness against this managing female."

"You better go to bed like she says, Ced," was Pa's advice. He kept his eye on Aunt Rose while he said it.

Aunt Rose reached behind her for a black iron frying pan that was sitting on the cold stove and came toward Uncle Ced and Pa. She had a wild look in her eye. "Look out, Ced!" Pa shouted. "Duck your head!"

I was scared now. Aunt Rose brought up her frying pan and brought it down on Uncle Cedric's head with a clang. It didn't seem to faze him one bit. After a moment he stood up real straight.

"Thank you, Rosie," he told her. "That was the unkindest cut of all. I'm going now, Rose. I'm going out of your life. You're going to have to beg my pardon for all the bad things you've done to me before I'll come back, and *if* I come back, I'll be boss here. You won't. I'm tired of feeling like two cents all the time."

He walked to the door. This was our chance. Pa and I followed him as fast as we could. Uncle Cedric turned around and opened the screen again. He stuck his head inside, letting the night moths, dozens of them, into the kitchen.

"I'm going to Joe's tonight. I don't know where I'll go from there, but I'm not coming back here. And don't you go taking it out on Hester. It's between you and me, Rose." He clicked his heels together and saluted her with his hand. "Good-by, General Perkins. Good-by to you!" He went down the steps like a king who'd just put on his crown for the first time and found it fit fine.

Aunt Rose didn't say a word. Leastwise, we couldn't hear any sounds from inside the kitchen.

It was a moonlight night and almost as bright as day. Whit got down from the wagon, and he and Pa helped Uncle Ced up. All of the other kids were sound asleep in the back.

"Ced's coming home with us," Pa explained to Mama.

She sighed. "I know it. We heard every word."

"It was awful in there, Whit," I told my brother, as we started for home. "Uncle Ced means it when he says he isn't going back."

Whit frowned. "That's a mess, all right. Hester, but what I got to tell you isn't so good, either. We didn't win even one race. A whole bunch of kids from Astoria won most of them. They must have been in training, too. They all had real long legs."

"Not even Clarrie?" I asked. I was surprised.

He shook his head. "Not even Clarrie. She fell down. Claimed it all came from wearing a dress and tight shoes. But Mama wouldn't let her take her shoes off."

"That's sure bad news, Whit," I agreed. We'd counted on that money to put us ahead.

The moon shone down on Uncle Ced. He was leaning on one elbow in the bottom of the wagon, singing, "We're tenting tonight on the old campground." After a while Mama and Pa began to pick up the tune and sing, too. Mama had a pretty voice, and so did Pa, who was the best square-dance caller in Washington Territory.

Whit and I didn't sing, even though we knew the words to that song. We didn't feel like it. I had fifteen cents in my pocket, tips I'd earned, to put in the secret place in the barn, the place we now called Ginty's Hole. That wasn't very much to add.

I looked back toward Ilwaco. It must have been ten o'clock. I saw a flash of light in the sky. Then came another and another. "It's the fireworks the grown-ups set off," Whit said.

"I know it." I looked away from the fireworks to see how Uncle Ced was doing. He'd stopped singing and was snoring, with his head on an old gunnysack. "I guess I've had enough fireworks of one kind or another for one day," I told my brother.

I didn't notice until we got down in front of our house that we didn't have Henry Bender anymore. Whit explained it to me. Pa had met a couple from Astoria in Ilwaco, and got to talking about horses with them. The man had been real taken with Henry Bender, while Pa fancied his little dapple gray, so they had traded horses right on the spot. The gray was called Manassas after a Civil War battle. His only fault was that he was something of a biter. Pa said it didn't matter. He liked the gray's gaits. The horse had style, and he knew how to break him of biting. He'd keep Manassas away from the other horses. He couldn't bite Prince or Maude if he was tied in his stall.

CHAPTER 7

Trouble

Uncle Ced was pale and shaky when he came down to breakfast with us. He didn't want any gravy and biscuits, either. He only wanted coffee. I'd ground it and parched it just right in the old oven that morning, although Pa had had to put the bolts back in the door twice to keep it on. The old stove was going to be a goner before long. I hoped it would hold out until Christmas.

"What are you going to do now, Ced?" Pa asked.

Uncle Ced shook his head. "I don't know, Joe. Guess I'll go to Ilwaco. The man who runs the livery stable there told me that if I wanted a job, he had one for me any time. There's a spare room over the Last Chance. I could live there, I suppose, but I won't go back to Rosie till she says she's sorry for treating me the way she does in front of folks."

I felt pretty low. I sure didn't want to go back to Aunt Rose either, not now. I was glad it was Monday and I had the day off.

After the berry picking was over for the day, I tagged along when Cameron and the others went to get Philip Amory. Philip was all ready for us. He was wearing a sweater and had a blanket over his knees. He looked pretty good to me. There was some pink in his face, and he was getting brown. Miss Lewis, Bessie, and Cameron helped him down the ramp while he worked the wheels with his hands.

When we were out of sight of the house on the plank road behind the dunes, Philip twisted around to talk to Cameron. "Where'll we go today, Cameron? Same place?" He grinned, the first time I had ever seen him do that.

"If you want to go there, Phil," said Cameron.

I didn't ask any questions. I just walked along with everybody else until we got to the place where the creek flowed into the ocean. Then Philip tossed the blanket off his knees. "Ready?" he called out to Clarrie.

Clarrie took the blanket and folded it up.

After that Cameron pushed Philip's wheelchair into a clump of huckleberry bushes, came out, and skinned off his overalls. I put my hands over my eyes, but Clarrie and Anna laughed, so I guessed it was all right. Cameron had on another pair underneath. He threw his top overalls into the bushes to Philip.

After a while Philip called out. "I'm ready! Come get me."

Cameron went into the bushes and brought Philip out. Philip had on the overalls, and he had taken off his shirt. He gave his silver watch to Clarrie to hold, and then my brother wheeled him right down to the edge of the creek. Philip raised himself up on the arms of his chair by his hands. Cameron put his arms out to hold Philip up and, as we all watched, he helped Philip out of the wheelchair and down into the brown water of the creek.

It was about four feet deep there, that was all. Cameron held Philip up in the running water until Philip grabbed hold of a branch down in the channel where the water ran fastest.

"Let go," Philip cried.

Cameron let him go, and Philip flopped down in the water all by himself. Cameron stood right by him. I noticed that Philip couldn't move his feet at all. He just let the water run over his legs.

Anna sat down on the bank. So did Clarrie, Tom, and Sarah. "Come on, Hester, sit down," Clarrie told me. "This'll take a while. It always does."

I sat down. "What's he doing?" I whispered to Clarrie.

"He says he's swimming."

"That isn't swimming!"

"We know that. Philip knows it, too, but he says it makes him feel good. He used to be a good swimmer back in Portland. He can still move his arms. Watch him!"

Now Cameron caught hold of the back of the overalls and held Philip up. He pulled him over to where the water ran slower, and Philip moved his arms the way people do in a breaststroke. He had to drag his legs and he didn't move fast, but he got to the bank all right.

After a while it wasn't much fun watching Philip and Cameron in the creek. They just did the same things over and over, although sometimes Philip put his face down in the water. I'd almost forgotten about the creek. The water was warm in the summer, and there were trees around it, so you couldn't get sunburned. We used to go in a lot last year, before we started earning money for the stove. There hadn't been much time for fun this summer.

"Time to go now," Clarrie said finally, looking at Philip's watch. She explained to me, "Philip has to get out and get dressed again right away. He doesn't want Miss Lewis to know about the swimming. He figures she'd tell him not to."

"Oh," was all I had to say.

Cameron got Philip out, and he and Clarrie helped him into the wheelchair. They went back into the bushes, and in a little while Philip was in his own clothes. Clarrie put his blanket over his legs and gave him his watch. Then we went back out into the sunshine. It was a hot day. Philip's hair would be dry by the time we got him home, so would Cameron's wet pants. Cameron squeezed the water out of the overalls Philip had worn and put them over a log to dry.

"He'll come back and get them," Anna told me. "Then he'll put both pairs on, and Mama won't know the difference."

"Is this what you do every day while I'm at the Palace Hotel?" I asked.

Anna and Clarrie nodded. "That's what Philip wants. But he doesn't want us to tattle on him. You mustn't tattle either."

"All right," I said. "I won't tell if that's what Philip wants." But I didn't tell my brothers or sisters what Dr. Alf had said about infantile paralysis and how there was no hope for that disease. If swimming made Philip happy, that was just fine with me.

When we got home again, Uncle Ced was still there. I'd thought he'd have left before, but he was out in our barn with Manassas. When Pa was going off to cut wood, Manassas had taken a nip at Prince's flank, and Pa had had to put liniment on Prince before he could leave. Manassas hadn't broken the skin much.

Cedric Perkins looked at Manassas. The dapple gray looked back at him out of the corner of his eye and skinned back his lips, showing his big yellow teeth. "I'm not so sure I'll like working in a livery stable, after all, Hester," said Uncle Ced. "Maybe I'll go to Astoria and find me a job in a store."

Just then Anna came running into the barn, all out of breath. "Aunt Rose is coming down the road. What'll we do? She's driving the hotel rig."

Uncle Ced got flustered as all get out. "If she's coming in the rig, she's got the horsewhip with her. It isn't true what they say about me in Nahcotta. She never horsewhipped me before—she only said she was going to someday. But it isn't much of a step to that from a frying pan. I'm going to hide myself, Hester. Tell me when she's gone."

That made sense. Our barn was a big one. It had good hiding places. "Get up in the loft quick," I said. It had taken Aunt Rose a long time to get up a head of steam, but I guessed she'd made it.

Uncle Cedric went up the ladder as fast as Whit could ever do it, for all he was forty years old, even older than Pa. Being scared made people step lively.

Anna was still at the barn door. "You go find Ginty and Jersey with Tom and Sarah," I told her. "Cameron and Clarrie will have to round up Mr. Hogan's cows." All of the other kids were in the barnyard. They knew Aunt Rose was coming, and when I said, "Shoo, get out of here, and don't talk to her about Uncle Ced. Bring home the cows," they shooed. Nobody wanted to stay.

Mama and I would have to deal with Aunt

Rose. I took a deep breath and went into the house. Mama was heating the flatirons in the iron heater on the old stove. She had her ironing sprinkled and ready to go.

"Aunt Rose is here," I said. "Anna told me she was coming, and I told Uncle Cedric where to hide himself in the barn. That's what he wanted. Don't tell Aunt Rose about him. Tell her he's gone away and you don't know where."

"Dear me," Mama sighed. "I hate telling lies to my own sister, but I suppose I have to. What a mess!" Aunt Rose banged on the front door, and Mama called out, "Come in."

She sure did come in. She had on her black silk bonnet and new yellow driving gloves, to keep her hands nice. She stopped at the doorway of the kitchen.

"Hello, Rose," said Mama, fitting the iron holder to the flatiron. She splashed a drop of water onto the iron. It sizzled just right. "How are you, Rose?"

"Mad!" said Aunt Rose. "Mad clear through! Where's Ced? What have you done with him? Don't lie to me, Estella. I know he was coming here. He told me so."

"I wouldn't lie to you." Mama began to iron one of Whit's shirts. "Ced was here in the house last night."

"So he's gone now." Aunt Rose jumped to the idea and Mama didn't tell her anything different.

"I don't know where Cedric planned on going. He wasn't quite sure, Rose."

Aunt Rose came across the room as Mama turned the shirt over and ironed the other sleeve. She plunked herself in a chair as if she owned our house. "Not very sociable, are you, Estella?" she snapped.

"You weren't asked to my house today, Rose," Mama said quietly.

Aunt Rose sniffled. She couldn't say that wasn't the truth. "Well, I've come to take Ced home."

Mama ironed the front of the shirt now. "I don't think Ced'll go just because you came after him." She looked at Aunt Rose and held up the iron. "He means it, Rose. You'll have to ask his pardon, in front of people so you can't go back on your word."

"He just wants to shame me!" said Aunt Rose. "He wants to make a fool out of me where everybody can hear it."

"If you want Cedric back, you've got to do it, though. You know him, Rose. He likes to feel big. I think it would be wise of you to get a hired man, so Ced won't have to do woman's work around the hotel. He knows they laugh at him in Nahcotta."

"Fiddlesticks! Nobody ever takes any notice of Ced!"

Mama began to iron again. She ironed the collar and back and put the shirt aside before she said anything. "Now that's what I mean, Rose—just what you said. Cedric wants people to notice him—everybody does. Most of all, he wants you to take some notice of him."

"How could I help but notice him last night? You saw him. He was disgusting." Aunt Rose took a handkerchief out of her reticule and dabbed at her eyes. The handkerchief had tatting lace around the edges, and it smelled of rose water. She sniffled. I was surprised.

"Men go to saloons when they're driven away from home. That's why Cedric went."

Tears ran out of Aunt Rose's eyes. I could hardly believe it, so I came closer to her to see if it was really happening.

"Get your Aunt Rose a cup of coffee, Hester," Mama told me.

I poured the coffee. It was good coffee— Uncle Ced had liked it—but it was weak by

Aunt Rose's ideas of what coffee ought to be.

Mama spoke to me again. "Go outside, Hester, and feed the chickens."

"We already fed them."

"Well, feed them again." I knew by that that she only wanted to get rid of me. I hated being got rid of.

Aunt Rose was still crying. "I miss having Cedric around. I couldn't sleep a wink all night for worrying about him."

"I know, Rose. . . ." I heard Mama begin, as I went outside. I sat down on the bottom step. They talked so low I couldn't hear a word they said, and I didn't dare move up any closer.

Pretty soon, though, I heard the front door shutting, and I ran around the side of the house. Aunt Rose was getting into her rig. It was a shiny black one. She saw me, too, and beckoned to me to come over to her. I went up, slow and careful, and she leaned down. "Hester, you're a good girl. You take care of your mama and look out for her these days. If you find out where your Uncle Cedric is, you let me know."

I said, "Yes, Ma'am," wondering what

she'd meant about Mama, and not meaning a word of it about tattling on Uncle Ced.

When she was gone, I went back to the barn and called up to the hayloft. "You can come down now."

Uncle Ced poked his head out. So did Willoughby. They must have been under the hay together. I guess the cat thought it was a game. Willoughby twitched his whiskers, and Uncle Ced put his moustache in shape with his fingers. He came down more slowly than he went up. "She come here after me?" he wanted to know. "What'd she say?"

I nodded. "She wants you to come home. She started to cry."

I thought he'd grin to hear that, but he didn't—I couldn't always understand grown-ups. He looked sad and let out a deep breath. "I'm just crazy about that woman, but I'm not going to back out of it now. No sirree, I'm not going to crawl for her or anybody else."

We went into the house, and he said good-by to Mama. He said he'd walk to Ilwaco, thanks. Pa had told him he could ride Manassas, but after looking at the dapple gray, he'd thought better of it.

After he left, I looked hard at Mama. She

seemed healthy to me. "Are you feeling all right, Mama?" I asked. I was worried.

"Of course, Hester," she said. "I feel just fine."

So I gave up on it.

Whit came home that night with a long face. He'd come into the storeroom after lunch and found Mr. Willard showing the Nickel-Plated Beauty to some summer people. We all gasped at that, but Whit said Mr. Willard had told him the summer folks were "only looking." It still upset us, though. We decided we'd go see Miss Pitchford right away.

After we went crabbing the next morning, Whit and I went to work while Cameron and Clarrie and the others walked over to Bert Hogan's, where our teacher boarded. They took our signed paper along and told Miss Pitchford what had happened.

Miss Pitchford read the paper, and then she decided to go to Nahcotta with the kids.

Whit was on an errand when they got to the general store, so Tommy ran over for me. I asked Aunt Rose if I could leave for a little while, and she said all right, so I lit out for the store, too, before she changed her mind.

Miss Jenny was breathing fire. She slapped our paper down on the counter under Mr. Willard's nose. "What's this about your showing the children's stove to summer people? I read this contract you signed with them."

Mr. Willard wasn't buffaloed easily. He leaned on his counter, grinning. "You just keep out of this, Jenny. That so-called contract was a joke. I can sell that stove to anybody I choose. Sure, I signed that piece of paper, to get these kids out of my store mostly, but it isn't legal. They're all underage—every one of them. It'd never hold up in court."

"Well, it'll hold up if I sign my name to it. I'm over twenty-one," she told him.

"Won't do any good, Jenny. You'd be signing too late. That paper was drawn up way last spring. It's dated."

Miss Pitchford tapped her foot and didn't say anything for a minute. Then she said, "Jacob, I don't know if what you tell me is true or not. I do know one thing, though— if you dare sell that stove to anyone, I'll spread the word all over the peninsula that you cheat little children. It'll hurt your business."

He was hopping mad now, too. His eyes

got narrower and meaner. "All right. I wasn't going to sell their stove anyhow. I'll wait till before Christmas, like I said, but if they don't come up with twenty-seven dollars by then, that stove goes to the highest bidder. I've had me a stomachful of the Kimballs."

"Twenty-seven dollars?" she asked, as if she couldn't believe her ears. "My memory tells me that the stove costs twenty-five dollars."

"So it does," Mr. Willard told her. "The extra two dollars is for storage charges."

"Jacob Willard," Miss Pitchford said slowly, dropping each word down like a sharp icicle, "I don't think I ever want to see you again." Our teacher's voice was so icy that my blood ran cold. She went on, looking right into Mr. Willard's eyes. "You make Simon Legree look like a saint." Miss Jenny turned around now. "Come along, children, I don't like it in here one bit!" With us Kimballs all around her, the teacher headed for the door, but she stopped there and pointed at Mr. Willard. "If you take this out on Whitney Kimball, Jacob Willard, I don't know what I'll do to you, but I promise you, you won't like it." And with her saying this, we all went outside. When Miss

Jenny got mad, she was a holy terror. She got cold mad—not at all the way Aunt Rose used to.

July ended. I thought it never would, though. We had eleven dollars to put in Ginty's Hole. We were getting there.

Aunt Rose and Mr. Willard didn't take it out on us. We figured they were afraid to. Uncle Cedric got a job at the livery stable in Ilwaco, and sometimes we saw him at our house for supper. He borrowed a saddle horse from his employer and came on out-of-the-way paths to see us, because he didn't want to go through Nahcotta and run into Aunt Rose.

By now Aunt Rose must have heard that Uncle Ced was in Ilwaco, but she didn't ask me about him and she never went down there to look him up. Uncle Ced didn't look so good. He used to be a snappy dresser, when Aunt Rose picked out his clothes, but he wasn't now. I think he slept in them. But he hadn't got into the clutches of "demon rum," which was what scared Mama. He took the pledge and swore off drinking in Ilwaco, and he kept to it.

Aunt Rose looked pretty much the same. She had her pride, but she was quiet these days. It was easier working for her, and sometimes she even said I'd done a good job.

We didn't know as much about Miss Jenny and Mr. Willard. Whit said he never saw her come into the general store anymore. Mr. Willard bought some new shirts with mauve stripes and changed his hair oil to one that smelled like lilacs. That was the only change in him. But most important of all, he didn't show the Nickel-Plated Beauty to anyone again.

We went clamming when the tide was low, and crabbing and fishing when it wasn't. The salmonberries were all gone. We sold raspberries from our garden, and in late July we began picking wild blackberries. Although that wasn't hard, I was glad I was still working at the Palace Hotel. Garter snakes crawled out on the vines to sun themselves among the berries, and I didn't like snakes at all.

Our blackberries sold well. The summer people made jam and jelly out of them, just the way Mama was doing. Things looked good for everybody until August fifth. Cameron and Clarrie were picking berries on a great big bush, so tall they couldn't see over the top of it, when they heard somebody talking. It was Vestal and Virgil Johnson, picking north of the beach marker.

Cameron put his bucket down. He told me he didn't say much. He just lit into Virgil with his fists. Virgil lost the fight, but as he went back south of the marker, he shook his fist at us Kimballs, and yelled, "You just watch out! We're going to get you good!"

We yelled back, "Ha, ha!" At least that's what Clarrie told me we said.

Cameron got a black eye out of it, and Virgil had a cut lip. Mama was sure upset. She hated to see fighting. Cameron told her it was because Virgil called him a name. I figured that was a fib, but he couldn't tell the truth to Mama.

"What did you call Virgil?" Mama asked.

"A dumb old Siwash!"

"Oh dear, that wasn't at all nice of you, Cameron. Mrs. Johnson is one of my very dearest friends. She's a fine Christian woman. Why can't you get along better with Virgil? He's such a nice boy. He's part Indian, that's true, but the Indians were here in America before the white people came. You should be proud to be Virgil's friend. He's a real first settler. He's a blue blood."

"Nope, he ain't," Cameron said. "I hit

him and cut his lip, and his blood was red just like everybody else's."

Pa laughed into his coffee cup. He needed something to cheer him up. Manassas had just taken a chunk out of Maude, the other workhorse.

My birthday was in the middle of August. Mama baked me a cake, a big yellow one, and covered it with whipped cream. I was thirteen now. I didn't get any presents, except new blue and yellow hair ribbons, but I didn't care. We didn't have money to give each other birthday presents every year, anyhow.

All of us kids, even Sarah and Tom, were allowed to sit up on the front porch and sing until the moon came up the night of my birthday. The honeysuckle was still in bloom. The vine covered one whole side of the porch, and smelled so sweet we could almost taste the honey.

Whit spoke up in the dark. "Guess there'll be eight of us next year."

"Eight?" I asked.

"Pa told me in the barn just before supper. There's going to be a new baby coming. It'll be here about New Year's."

"A boy or a girl?" Sarah asked. "I want a girl. What'll it be, Hester?"

"You take what you get when it comes to babies," I told her. "Nobody knows what it'll be." Whit's news explained a lot of things I'd wondered about—the doctor's coming to see Mama a couple of times, saying he was merely "wandering by," Mama's tonic, and Aunt Rose's remarks that I hadn't understood.

"Nobody told me," said Cameron.

"Me neither," said Clarrie. "Did you know, Hester?"

"Now that you say so, Whit, I guess I did." I didn't talk to Clarrie directly, because I wasn't telling the truth, but I was the oldest girl, and I had to know more things than she did.

"That's real nice about a baby," Tom put in.

"Can the baby play with me?" Sarah asked quietly, snuggling up to me.

"Bound to play with you, Sarah," I told her.

Just then the moon came up right over the sand dunes. It was big and golden, almost a harvest moon. I shivered. Autumn was on its way.

Jerry came around the corner of the porch.

He put his paws on the bottom step and whined. His eyes were very sad in the moonlight. They looked wet. "I guess Pa must have told Jerry. Look at him," I said. "He seems to know he's going to have another one hanging onto his fur. He always knows."

Whit wasn't a lot happier than Jerry. "Wonder if Pa told Mr. Willard about it yet. You ought to see the bill we've run up at the general store by now. Hope he doesn't cut off Pa's credit. Those railroad men had better get here quick. Babies cost money."

I thought about that, and I thought about the stove, too. With the new baby coming, even if the railroad men came tomorrow and paid Pa and Pa paid Mr. Willard off, Pa couldn't help us out with the stove—if we ever told him about it. Well, I didn't want to have to tell him or Mama. I wanted it to be a surprise, the biggest surprise they ever had.

CHAPTER 8

Square Dance at Nahcotta

The purplish-blue huckleberries were ripe by the end of August, so we picked them when the blackberries were gone. It was hard work, because they were little and we had to pick a long time to get a pail of them. We upped the price to a dime a bucket, and were careful not to get any twigs or leaves in the pail, so we wouldn't lose our customers. I was surprised when Aunt Rose bought huckleberries with leaves in them from Vestal Johnson. I thought she'd throw a fit, but she didn't. She only picked out the leaves and threw them away.

Aunt Rose had sure changed. She was moping. She asked me about Uncle Cedric a couple of times, wanting to know if I'd seen him. When I didn't tell her anything, she gave up asking. I caught her crying once while she helped me peel the onions for the beef stew she was making for the paying guests' supper. She'd helped me peel onions before Uncle Ced walked out, and it hadn't fazed her a bit.

It was always quiet in the kitchen now, except for the times Uncle Alf came in to talk to me. Aunt Rose didn't light into him, either, the way she used to.

Uncle Alf and I were talking one day while Aunt Rose was in the dining room setting the tables for lunch. "Did you see Uncle Ced at Ilwaco? How is he?" I asked. We hadn't seen him at Ocean Park for two weeks.

"Yes, I saw him, Hester. He doesn't look so good to me."

"Is he sick?" I asked. "Mama's afraid he'll take to drink."

"No, he isn't sick—not the sort of sickness that would call me in. He's just moping."

I understood. "Like Aunt Rose," I said.

"Yes." Dr. Alf sighed. "They're both as stubborn as mules. I don't know how it's going to end. From his appearance, Ced isn't eating regularly, and it can't be because he's not making any money. He tells me he's doing quite well."

"Aunt Rose isn't eating, either. She didn't eat her lunch yesterday or the day before."

"Blasted fools! They'll really need my services the way they're going on. Neither of them will give an inch. I guess someone else will have to take a hand. I'd do it myself if I didn't know I'd get it bitten off at the elbow."

That made me think of Mr. Willard and Miss Pitchford. I sort of hoped, now that Mr. Willard didn't seem to be in the running anymore, that Uncle Alf would get in the race himself and court our teacher.

When Dr. Alf walked out of the kitchen, Aunt Rose met him at the swinging door. "Alf," she asked, her voice low, "you seen Ced lately?"

"Yes, I have, Rose." He waited for her to go on, watching her.

She looked down at her apron and smoothed it out with her fingers. "I know he's at the livery stable," she went on. "How is he?"

"As well as can be expected, under the circumstances," he told her. "He hasn't taken to rum or whiskey, if that's what you mean, but he revels in that vile weed tobacco. And he's holding to his word. He won't come home until you apologize in public—and that's just plain silly. There isn't a soul on the peninsula who doesn't know that you're sorry. You haven't taken the hide off anybody's back for a whole six weeks." Uncle Alf jammed his hat on his head and stomped out. He'd said his piece, and it left me gasping.

Aunt Rose started to cry. She put her apron up over her face and went right across the kitchen and out the back door. She didn't come back for half an hour.

That was when I decided I'd take a hand in helping my aunt and uncle out—even if I did get it bitten off, the way Uncle Alf said. I decided at the same time that I'd better give up on him and Miss Pitchford. Uncle Alf was a hard nut to crack. He'd probably meant it that time he said he didn't take to schoolmarms.

By the first of September we had sixteen dollars and twenty-three cents in Ginty's Hole. That left about eleven dollars for us to earn. The huckleberries were getting harder to find. Clarrie, Cameron, Tom, and Anna had begun to pick in the shady places, where the berries were the last to get ripe. They took Sarah along with them all the time now. She was small enough to get at the berries where they grow low down, and she could squeeze inside the bushes. It was about time Sarah did a little work, we decided. She was six years old now.

Whit had gone to see Mr. Ross, the man who owned the cranberry bog. Mr. Ross said he'd hire the six of us Kimballs on Saturdays when the berries were ready to be picked. If we were going to make up Mr. Willard's twenty-seven dollars, we'd have to get going on the cranberries. The summer people would be leaving at the end of the first week of September, and that would cut off our clam and crab and berry money all at once. Maybe we could sell oysters later on, but that was in the future.

I didn't let on to the others, but I was getting worried that maybe we wouldn't make it. Aunt Rose had already told me she was letting me go the fourth of September. That was when the old folks at the Palace Hotel all packed up and went home on the *Harvest Queen*.

And that was when school started.

Something nice happened when we came home on the first day of school. "You all go out to the barn," Mama told us. "There's a surprise for you."

"Willoughby had kittens!" Sarah said.

"Silly!" Clarrie snapped at her. "Willoughby's a tomcat. He's a boy."

"I wanted kittens," said Sarah. She was sure stubborn.

"It's not kittens. Go look."

We all threw our schoolbooks down on the kitchen table and ran out the back door. There was a real surprise in the barn, all right. Manassas was gone. Pa had traded him off that morning. There were two horses in his stall now. One was a pretty little bay mare with a black mane and tail. Beside her was a long-legged colt. It was a spring colt, and it looked just like the mare.

Sarah and Tom jumped up and down, they were so happy. "Can we ride him? Can we ride him now?" Sarah wanted to know.

Mama had come out to the barn with us. "The mare is Belinda," she said. "The colt is hers. I'm sorry, but you can't ride him. He isn't big enough yet, and he hasn't been broken. He's never had a bit in his mouth."

"What's the colt's name?" Anna asked.

"He doesn't have one yet," Mama told us. "You'll have to name him."

That was exciting. We sat on the hay bales in the barn and thought up names until it was time to do our chores. We finally settled on Albert, because Mr. Albert Wagner, who came in the summers, had brown eyes a lot like the colt's. Then I thought we ought to have a middle name for the colt. All of us had middle names. We considered it some more, and after we'd argued a lot, we named the colt Albert William.

Tommy threw his arms around Albert William's neck as soon as we had decided what he'd be called. "I sure like you, Al," he said.

"All that name-thinking-up work for nothing," I had to say, but nobody listened, as usual.

Everybody at school wanted to come see Albert William, but we were choosy. We wouldn't let just anybody see him. Cameron wanted to charge a penny a look, but I didn't think we ought to make money off our friends. That wasn't right. Summer folks were different.

We didn't ask Vestal or Virgil to see Albert William. We didn't want them around our place. We knew it made them mad, because they did a bad thing one day. Virgil had saved up a string of ladyfinger firecrackers from the Fourth of July celebration, and he lit it and threw it at our dog Jerry. Jerry jumped right up into the air and ran home. He hid under the back porch for three whole days, he was that afraid. When there was a baby coming, we thought that was a mean thing to do to old Jerry.

Another thing happened to us in September. It was a good thing. The railroad men finally got to Ocean Park. They measured Pa's wood and paid him. Pa paid off the helpers he'd had all year, and then he went to the general store and paid Mr. Willard off, too. There wasn't much money left after those things had been taken care of. There wasn't enough for Pa to ask Mr. Willard about buying a new stove for Mama, so our secret was still safe.

With school on we couldn't take Philip Amory swimming anymore, but Cameron went over to push him around on the beach after school every day just the same. Cameron was sorry to see Philip go away, and not just because of the money we were losing. They really liked each other a lot.

The last day Philip was to be in Ocean Park, Cameron had a good idea. "Let's take old Albert William over to Philip's house."

"What'll the judge say?" I wanted to know.

"Oh, he won't care. We ain't going to bring Albert William inside the house."

I went with Cameron, Clarrie, Tom, Anna, and Sarah to say good-by to Philip, even if I didn't know him very well. I wanted another look at the judge, too. I didn't know when I'd ever see anybody so elegant again.

Cameron led Albert William. Maybe the rest of us didn't look so grand when we went up to the Benton place, but there wasn't any reason to be ashamed of Albert William. He had been groomed and curried until he glittered, and my brother had braided one of Clarrie's red hair ribbons into his tail. Clarrie didn't care about things like hair ribbons. I'd sure have had something to say to Cameron if he'd asked for one of mine.

Philip was on the front porch the way he always was, when we got there, and the judge came out, too. Those people were sure great porch sitters. We never had the time. And my, wasn't the judge elegant! He was dressed all in pearl gray, and his waistcoat had the prettiest silver threads in it. I couldn't take my eyes off him. He nodded to all of us and then came down the steps to look at Albert William. He pried open the colt's mouth, just as if Albert William was a big horse. "Fine animal," Judge Amory said.

Cameron nearly burst, he swelled up so much. "He's mine," he told the judge. "I'm going to break him."

That was a great big whopper of a lie, and we all put our hands over our mouths. It didn't bother Cameron, though. He kept on grinning, the fibber.

The judge just nodded. "Well, he's a nice colt. I'm glad you brought him over. I want to thank you for taking Philip out for a stroll each day."

"He sure liked going swimming," said Tommy, as loud as he could. "He liked that better than strolling."

Cameron let go of Albert William's hack-amore. The colt jumped, and Cameron caught him again just before he got away. My brother was really mad now. "You went and tattled again, Tommy!"

We all stared at Philip next. He had sort of shrunk in his wheelchair. His father's mouth had flopped open. Tommy had sure let the cat out of the bag this time.

The judge looked from the six of us to Philip and back to us again. Miss Lewis, who had been sitting on the porch, too, got up. She had her hand over her heart and was hanging onto the post. "Oh, dear!" she cried out. "I didn't know about this."

The judge bent his head and looked into Cameron's face. I wondered if he did that to robbers in Portland when they were on trial for their wicked crimes. "Did I hear you say you took Philip swimming?" His voice was peculiar.

Cameron was brave. He stood up to the judge. "Yes, sir, I did. That's what he wanted to do."

"Then this was your idea, Philip." Judge Amory turned to his own boy. He was looking daggers at Philip now, too.

"Yes, sir," Philip said to his father.

"I'll deal with you later," the judge told him.

"Is he going to get a licking? Will Philip have to go to the woodshed?" Anna whispered to me, but I was too scared to answer her.

The cat finally let go of my tongue, and I spoke up. "We didn't mean anything by it, Judge Amory, honest we didn't. It made Philip happy to go swimming, and he looks better than he did when you first brought him up here."

That was true. Even sitting all scrooched up in his wheelchair, Philip looked good.

"You can't send us all to jail," Cameron said right out to the judge. "The little kids just went along to watch. It was all my doing. Besides, my sister's right. Philip's better than he was."

The judge fastened onto that like a dog onto a barn rat. "What do you mean—better?"

Cameron called out to Philip, "You show him, Phil!"

"But I was going to show him later on," Philip said. He wasn't smiling, but he wasn't as scared as he had been.

"You better show him right now."

Philip threw off his blanket. It landed down in the red dahlias below the porch. We watched him lean down and take off his shoes. He had brown socks on. Philip made an awful face, and then, while everybody looked at his feet, he wiggled first the toes of one foot and then the other.

I was disappointed. What was so all-fired fancy about that?

But Judge Amory and the nurse didn't seem to think the way I did. They looked as if somebody had dropped a horse collar on them. I could tell by their faces they couldn't believe it. "Philip, can you do that again?" his father asked.

Now Philip grinned. "I sure can!" He wiggled his toes again.

"Philip!" The judge was up on the porch in a minute, and he hugged Philip right in front of us. "Wait until we see those doctors in Portland now!"

"That's all I can wiggle," Philip said.

"It's a wonder. It's a miracle! Perhaps you'll improve some more."

"Aw, it was only swimming," Cameron said, disgusted. "Come on, let's take Albert William home. Good-by, Phil."

"Come back here, young man!" The judge fished in his vest pocket and brought out a three-dollar gold piece. We'd never seen one before. It was yellow and bright, about the size of a dime, but a lot thinner. The judge gave the gold piece to Cameron. "This is for making my boy's toes wiggle again, and for all the work you must have done."

"Why, thanks," said Cameron. "I didn't do much but hold Philip up in the water. He did all the work himself. He could do it in any creek with anybody."

I was sure happy when Cameron took the money. That was over nineteen dollars now for Ginty's Hole. And I'd been worried we couldn't make it!

"Now, children, tell me," the judge asked. "What are you going to do with the money you've worked so hard for all summer? And come have some lemonade and cake on the porch with us."

"Shall we tell him, Hester?" Clarrie asked.

I thought hard. He was a judge. People shouldn't lie to judges. I'd tell him.

So we all sat down, except Albert William—we tied him to the porch post. I was the oldest one there, so I told the judge and Miss Lewis all about the Nickel-Plated Beauty while we ate cake. I didn't have to worry about Bessie's blabbing our secret. She'd gone back to high school.

The judge nodded and nodded, but he only said, "Well, now, that's a very commendable and ambitious project." I wasn't quite sure what that meant, but by the way the judge's voice sounded, it wasn't bad.

We remembered our manners. We finished every crumb of the cake and every bit of the lemonade, and when Sarah, who was the slowest, was through, we all got up and said, "Thank you" to the judge. Then, when Judge Amory stuck out his hand, we shook it, every one of us, and Miss Lewis's hand and Philip's hand, too. Miss Lewis seemed a little surprised. I had forgotten ladies didn't shake hands.

We untied Albert William and left, but we stopped on the top of a sand dune and waved and yelled, "Good-by, Philip." After that we all went home. Summer was really over now.

We did a lot of talking about Philip Amory after he went back to Portland. We hoped he'd come back next year. I was still surprised at how excited the grown-ups got when Philip wiggled his toes, and once, when Mama sent me to the store at Nahcotta to buy some white flannel to make gowns for the baby, I stopped Uncle Alf, who was driving his buggy, and asked him about it.

"It's about the summer boy, Philip Amory," I said, patting Dr. Alf's old mare. "When Philip went home, he could move his toes."

"Well, that's fine news. I wonder what did it."

"Cameron took him swimming all summer."

"Well, if swimming did the boy any good, it was the right thing, wasn't it? There's nothing like exercise. I hope the lad keeps on with his swimming. There are natatoriums in Portland. Can't see a bit of harm in it." Dr. Alf tipped his hat to me, just as if I was a grown-up in long skirts with my hair up on top of my head every day. He called out to his horse, "Get along now, Rosinante."

His horse's name always made me grin. Aunt Rose hated it. I guess she thought the doctor was making fun of her when he called his horse that, but he told me once that it was the name of a knight's horse in an old story from Spain.

After I got the flannel I went over to the Palace Hotel. Aunt Rose was sitting in the kitchen all alone. Only one stove had any fire in it. The others would be cold until next summer. I felt sorry for Aunt Rose. She looked peaked.

She was glad to see me, almost as if I'd been a grown-up caller, and said, "Well, look who's here." Then she asked me about Mama's condition and about the railroad men's coming and all about Philip Amory and us. She asked me next if I'd sent away to Montgomery Ward for that dress I wanted. She wanted to know what it looked like and what color it was going to be—blue or red.

I didn't want to lie again to Aunt Rose, so I came right out with the truth about the Nickel-Plated Beauty. I told her about all our hard work in the summer and how we were going to pick cranberries later on, too. I even told her how much money we had.

She was sure surprised. "Well, that's fine, Hester. I wasn't fair to you when I said you just wanted to work here to earn money for fine feathers, was I?"

"No, Ma'am," I said.

"Your mama is very lucky to have you children. I'll keep your secret," she told me. She got up to pour herself a cup of coffee and to get a glass of cool milk from the pantry for me. "Estella must be proud of such a fine family," Aunt Rose said. She looked around at her kitchen, as if she were counting up pots and pans and dishes and silver coasters in her head. She let out a sigh when she looked at her three stoves.

"You have three stoves, Aunt Rose. You're rich," I told her. I thought that would make her feel better.

"I don't know about that, Hester." She folded her hands on the kitchen table. "I get mighty lonesome here sometimes all by myself. It's a long time till summer comes." She changed the subject. "Is your pa going to do the calling at the square dance on the twenty-fifth?"

"Yes'm, he's planning to. They're going to pay him a whole two dollars for it."

"Calling's hard work," Aunt Rose said. She looked at her wall calendar, the one showing a fat lady in a white dress, leaning up against a big vase and looking sad. "The twenty-fifth is Ced's and my wedding anniversary. We've been married fifteen years. I ordered a new dress before Cedric went away, and it came last month in the mail. I thought maybe we'd go to Astoria overnight on our anniversary, after the summer people went home, but it just didn't work out that way."

"Will you come to the dance, Aunt Rose?"

"I don't think so, Hester. There isn't much point to it."

"Uncle Alf'd take you."

Her eyes flashed fire. "Well, I sure won't be asking him! Even if he took me, he'd be running off to look at a sore big toe somebody stepped on."

And that was the end of that. She didn't offer to show me the new dress. I wanted her to go to the harvest dance, though, because I'd heard Pa say to Mama that Uncle Ced was going to be there.

We were going to the dance, every one of us. Of course, Sarah and Tom would fall asleep right off, but there would be beds made up for all the little kids, and even for us bigger ones. Sometimes folks danced until four or five o'clock in the morning on the Saturday night of the harvest dance. The circuit preachers must have known about it, because they never showed up in Nahcotta the Sunday after the dance. The next Sunday, though, they generally had plenty to say about it.

It took us Kimballs all day to get ready. Everybody got bathed and combed and dressed up as fine as he could. I had on my yellow muslin and wore yellow ribbons in my hair. I helped Mama get ready, too, and held the tongs of the curling iron over the chimney of the kerosene lamp until they got hot. Then I curled her hair. We girls all admired Mama's hair, wishing that there was something to uncurl our curls so we'd look the same.

"I wish we had Whitney hair, Mama," said Anna.

"So do I," I said.

Mama just laughed at us. "I think you have lovely hair—all of you. And you're very lucky. You don't have to use kid-leather curlers or rags the way most girls do, you know."

That was true, but we still didn't agree.

Pa filled the wagon with hay and hitched

up Prince and Maude. I snuggled down next to Sarah. My, I was excited! We kept stopping to pick up other people, and they were excited, too. When we went by the Johnson house I saw that the lights were still on there. Mama told us that Mrs. Johnson hadn't been feeling well and that maybe the Johnsons wouldn't be going to the dance after all.

When we got to the general store, we saw other carriages and wagons already there. People came from twenty miles around to the harvest dance. We could hear the fiddler tuning up, getting his notes from the piano.

Pa helped us all down after he tied Prince and Maude. Our pa was an important man tonight, because he was the caller. Without a caller to tell the dancers what to do next, there couldn't be a square dance. We walked through all the people, and some of them called out to Pa.

The hall on top of Mr. Willard's store was half full already. It was a good thing it was a big place. There was a platform at one end for the people who played the fiddles, the piano, and the concertina. Pa went up and started to talk to them about what they were to play. I put our coats and shawls away on a big table in the corner. Now that Pa was here it was close to starting time.

Cameron, Clarrie, Anna, and the little kids went crazy, of course. They ran around the hall, chasing each other and the other kids. I sat down beside Mama.

"I think we'll have a nice crowd here tonight," Mama said, loosening her shawl. She frowned a little then. "I do hope there won't be too much going on outside."

I nodded my head. I knew what she was talking about. Dancing was hot work. Some of the men thought it was thirsty work, too. They headed for the back stairs a lot. Some of them had jugs in their hay wagons.

Then Mama sighed and pointed at the floor. "Look at those. Just count them, Hester."

I counted. There were twenty-two cuspidors along the walls. They expected a lot of tobacco chewing tonight.

Just then some more people came in. They were laughing and talking, and some of them talked to Mama and me before they put their coats away. At the tail end of all these folks was Uncle Ced. He looked better than he had for a long time. He had on a new dark-gray suit and a waistcoat with blue flowers on it. There was a lady with him, a big stout lady in purple satin. She had blackish-brown hair and jet earrings and a Spanish comb in her hair. I never saw anybody so bugled, buttoned, and bangled before. Even the ruffles on the back of her bustle had ruffles on them.

"I don't believe it!" Mama said under her breath. "What will Rose say?"

"Uncle Ced's got another woman!" I gasped.

Mama stiffened up, and her face went white. Uncle Ced was coming right to us, bold as brass. The stout lady wore violet-smelling perfume. Everybody turned around and sniffed the air as she went by.

"Good to see you, Estella," said my uncle, just as if everything was all right. "I want you to meet somebody I brought up from Ilwaco with me." Mama and I were speechless. This was a terrible thing. But Uncle Ced went right on. "I want you to know Miss Essie Akerman, Estella. She's come to the dance with Jake Willard. He didn't think he could get closed up in time to get to Ilwaco for her, so I brought Essie along with me. Can she wait for Jake here with you?"

"Pleased to meet you." Miss Akerman, who was tall, stopped to look down at Uncle Ced. "I'm sorry, Mr. Perkins, but I didn't catch the lady's name."

"It's Mrs. Kimball." Mama let out her breath as if a pin had been stuck in her. We were sure glad to hear that Mr. Willard was escorting the lady from Ilwaco. If Aunt Rose got wind that Uncle Ced was with another lady, there was no telling what might happen. She might burn down the hall.

Mama spoke up just fine now. "This is my oldest daughter, Hester." Then she said low to me, "Hester, you get up. Give Miss Akerman your seat. And go make Clarrie stop running around so much. She's too big to act like that."

I got up. With a rustle of taffeta petticoats, Miss Akerman sat down in the chair I'd barely begun to warm and started to talk to Mama about the Eagle Grill in Ilwaco, where she was a waitress.

Uncle Ced was left out of things. He stood around for a little while next to Mama, and then he headed for the platform. I guessed he wanted to say hello to Pa. Nobody was paying any attention to him, and I felt sorry for him. Even among all those people he looked lonesome. He kept glancing hopefully all around him, but nobody said anything to him.

I caught up with Clarrie and told her what Mama had said. Then I grabbed my chance.

Mama wasn't watching me. I made it to the back door, looked just once over my shoulder as the music started for the first dance—a Virginia reel—and ran down the steps right by three men who had a jug out already. I headed straight for the Palace Hotel.

I pushed open the back door without even knocking. Aunt Rose was at the kitchen table with her spectacles on and the wish book open in front of her. "Uncle Ced's at the dance," I told her.

"Is he, Hester?" she said, taking off her spectacles.

I took a deep breath. "He's with another lady," I lied.

"He is!" Aunt Rose sat up very straight.

"Yes'm. I came to get you."

"Well, I'll go right over and see about this." She was the old Aunt Rose now, and breathing fire.

"No, don't," I told her. "That lady's wearing a purple-satin dress and violet-smelling perfume. She's got on taffeta petticoats. I heard them when she sat down to talk to Mama."

"Your mother, my own sister, is talking to a scarlet woman?"

"Yes, Ma'am, I guess she is, but the lady's dress is purple. I just told you."

Aunt Rose started for the door, but then she stopped, the way I'd hoped she would. "Purple dress, taffeta petticoats? That what you said, Hester?"

"That's what I said, Aunt Rose."

"You get right upstairs with me, Hester. Take the lamp. I'll get the curling iron. We'll show that hussy a thing or two. This is a game that two can play at. I'll teach Ced."

"Yes'm."

I followed Aunt Rose with the lamp. I wanted to laugh, but I didn't dare. I helped curl her red hair, too, pulled the strings of her corset as tight as I could pull them and she could stand it, and then fastened the hooks in her new dress for her. It was as pretty as could be—crystal-blue taffeta, with a bustle, an elegant polonaise, and Chantilly lace at the cuffs and around the top. It rustled all by itself just like leaves in the wind. She had two taffeta petticoats on underneath, a black one and a wine-red one, and she wore French kid shoes with high heels and tassels. I didn't know Aunt Rose had clothes like that.

She looked in the mirror while she put on

her garnet earrings and her garnet brooch. Then she turned to me. "Hester, if you breathe a word of this, I'll tell your mother about the stove at the general store. Go get me the red flannel. It's in the top dresser drawer. I'll bet that hussy paints her face."

I watched as Aunt Rose wet the flannel and rubbed the red stain into her cheeks and on her lips. Then she bit her lips. The last thing she did was dab rice powder on her face.

"Desperate situations call for desperate remedies, Hester. Never forget that. Always keep a scrap of red flannel handy when you grow up." She dashed some drops of Florida water on her handkerchief. "Drat this namby-pamby eau de cologne. Next time I go to Portland I'm buying me some perfume from Paris, France. I just wish I had some heliotrope now. Violet indeed!" She turned around to look at me. "Well, do I pass inspection? How do I look?"

I was so surprised I couldn't do anything except gulp and say, "Just fine, Aunt Rose." She looked more than fine, though. She was downright pretty. "You look better than she does," I told her.

Aunt Rose didn't smile. "Well, Hester,

let's go," she said, grabbing up her pretty black-lace fan.

I hoped she wasn't going to hit Essie Akerman or Uncle Ced with the fan, but I guessed it couldn't hurt anybody much, except for its enamel handle.

General Perkins and I went out of the Palace Hotel like greased lightning. This was war, but I didn't feel very brave at all. What would Aunt Rose say when she learned the truth about Miss Akerman from Ilwaco? I was scared to think about it.

There was no back door for Aunt Rose, no sirree! We came in the front, big as life, pushing by people who were late. Pa had begun to call the fourth square dance. The music makers were playing an old song, "Weevily Wheat," and Pa was calling out, "Gents to the center in a Texas star." Four of the men went to the center of each square and put up their right arms high and moved around. Aunt Rose and I stood by the door while the dancers do-si-doed or dived for the oyster and dived for the clam when Pa told them to.

"Where is she?" Aunt Rose asked me, her eyes on the dancers.

I pointed to the third square. Miss Akerman and Mr. Willard, who was all dressed up in a brown suit and a yellow waistcoat, were partners. Uncle Ced was in the same square partnering, believe it or not, Clarrie! Mama was sitting alone, tapping her foot. She wasn't going to dance much tonight. Uncle Alf had told her not to. The rest of us Kimballs were running all over the place again, but then so was everybody else who wasn't grownup yet.

Aunt Rose went over to the empty chair next to Mama and sat down. She kept staring at Mr. Willard and the lady in purple. Miss Akerman was a good dancer. Mr. Willard wasn't, but he kept trying.

"Who's that, Estella—the fat, overdressed one in purple?" Aunt Rose's voice was funny, as if she was panting.

"That's Essie Akerman. How nice you look tonight, Rose! We're so glad to see you here," said Mama, changing the subject.

Aunt Rose snorted. "I'll just bet you are. I hear that Ced came here with a shameless woman, a home wrecker."

Mama looked at me over Aunt Rose's head. I looked down at my shoes. Mama was sure a good guesser.

"So he did, Rose, but he only drove Miss Akerman up here as a favor to Mr. Willard.

Mr. Willard really asked her to the dance. Miss Akerman tells me she and Mr. Willard have an understanding."

"She's his intended then?"

"Yes, Rose, she is."

Aunt Rose sort of sagged in her chair. "Oh, dear, Estella, I got the wrong idea. If I'd known, I'd never have come over here."

"I can guess who gave you that idea," Mama said, giving me a sharp look.

The music ended, and Pa yelled out, "Next one's a waltz, folks. It's a ladies' choice."

"Now, Rose Whitney," said Mama, "you listen to me—even if it is the first time in your life you ever did. Here's your chance. It's a ladies' choice waltz. You go choose Cedric right now. You better get there first, too. If you don't, somebody else will. Ced's a fine man and you could lose him."

Aunt Rose got up. She looked at her fan for a minute while she bit her lips some more. Then she said, "I'm going to do it. I'm going to do it."

When the square dancers started to take partners for the waltz, Aunt Rose went across the floor under a full head of steam, her fan folded and dangling from her wrist. Everybody got out of her way. Clarrie, standing by Uncle Ced, took one look at her and skedaddled, scared.

Aunt Rose looked really pretty. I believed now what they said about her when she was a girl—that she jumped horses bareback, except for a cinch, through hoops of fire, to win prizes at county fairs. She had lots of grit.

So did Uncle Ced. He stood his ground, even when she came to a halt right in front of him.

Everybody in the hall was looking at her, and had been ever since she came in the front door, but it didn't faze Aunt Rose a bit. "Cedric Perkins," she said, her voice ringing out like a bell, "I'm sorry. Will you dance with me?"

He gave her his arm. "Glad to, Rosie," he said loudly. Then he swung her off into the "Tales of the Vienna Woods" waltz. Neither he nor Aunt Rose had eyes for anybody else. I guessed I'd be forgiven for what I did.

Everybody waltzed, even Clarrie and Pa, but I didn't see anyone but Aunt Rose and Uncle Ced. Mama wiped her eyes on the hem of her shawl. "Never thought I'd see the day Rose's pride would bend," she told me, just as if I'd been a grown-up.

CHAPTER 9

Disaster Strikes

It was sure some dance. I danced a lot, too, later on, with some nice boys from Oysterville. Even though I got tired, I was mighty pleased with myself.

We were all invited to stay overnight at the Palace Hotel. Aunt Rose and Uncle Ced wouldn't let us refuse, although we'd planned to stay at somebody else's place. Pa knew he'd have to call until the sun came up, but the rest of us went over to the hotel at eleven o'clock.

At six o'clock in the morning Pa came and got us up. We couldn't stay for breakfast. The chores had to be done, the chickens fed, and Ginty and Jersey put out to pasture.

When Pa drove into our barnyard, Virgil Johnson came streaking out of our barn and right across the sand dunes like a scalded pup, with Red and Jerry running alongside him.

"Go get Virgil, Whit," I yelled out, but I didn't need to tell my brother that. He left the wagon in a flash, lighting out after Virgil.

I was so surprised that I didn't move until I heard Virgil yelling from the other side of the dunes. Whit must have caught him. "Ginty's Hole!" I whispered to Clarrie. "I'm going to the barn right now. I want to see about our money!"

"Hey, what's going on, kids?" Pa croaked at us like an old bullfrog. He always came near to losing his voice when he called the square dances all night. We were jumping out of the wagon on all sides. Clarrie and Cameron and Tom went over the sand dunes as fast as they could go. Anna had heard me talking to Clarrie in the wagon about Ginty's Hole, and she and I headed for the barn. Only Sarah, who was half asleep, stayed in the wagon with Mama.

I threw the board off Ginty's Hole, and Anna and I went down on our knees in our best clothes. I pawed the dirt away, so we could see if the old salt sack was still there. The blue bandanna couldn't hold all of our money anymore, and we kept it in the salt sack now, so it wouldn't fall out in the dirt and get lost. It was still there, praise be! I could see the white cloth.

Anna and I let out deep breaths and got up. "Come on," I told her, "let's tell the others, and let's find out why Virgil was sneaking around here."

We left the barn just as Whit came over the top of the dune, holding Virgil by the straps of his overalls. Cameron had him by the arm. The dogs were jumping and barking and trying to put their paws on Virgil. Red licked Virgil's face. That made me mad at Red, all right.

"What's wrong?" Mama asked from the wagon.

"Virgil was sneaking around our house," Whit told her.

"But why would you do a thing like that, Virgil?" Mama wanted to know. Virgil looked up at her, and then he began to bawl. "Whitney, Cameron, let go of him!" My brothers stepped back, even if they didn't like it. "Now you tell me, Virgil, what were you doing in our barn?"

"I came to see the colt, Mrs. Kimball," Virgil blubbered. "I never did get to see him. Everybody else at school did." He pointed to Cameron. "He and the rest of your kids wouldn't let me and Vestal see Albert William."

"You haven't seen Albert William?" Mama asked him. Her voice was soft, the way it was when she tucked the little kids in for the night.

"No, Ma'am, but I got a look at him just before you came home."

"Well, it's a pity, Virgil, that you didn't see him before. I'm sorry about this. I didn't know about it. You tell Vestal to come over here this afternoon. Clarrie will be happy to show Albert William to her."

"Oh, Mama!" Clarrie wailed.

Mama just gave Clarrie one look. That was enough.

Virgil said, "I'll tell her, Mrs. Kimball. I'll sure tell her." Then he was gone, heading lickety-split for home.

Pa helped Mama and Sarah down. Mama didn't look so pleased. "We're all going to have a talk after breakfast," she said. "Something's going on here, and I don't like it."

She held Sarah's hand while they went in the back door. Pa told Whit to unhitch Prince and Maude and put out some hay for them. I hung around until Pa had gone inside, too.

"Why do you suppose old Virgil was hanging around here?" Clarrie asked.

"He didn't come to see Albert William." Anna was sure of that.

"He was up to no good." Cameron shook his head. "I wish I'd got to hit him again, but he's a squirmer when you get him down."

Tom put into words what we all thought. "Yep, he's a bawler, too. I think he came over here to our place to steal the stove money."

"He could do it," Whit put in. "Red and Jerry would take a piece out of anybody they didn't know, but they weren't chasing Virgil when he lit out of the barn. They were running with him, like our chasing him was sort of a game."

I hadn't said anything much, but now I sighed. "I guess we're sure going to catch it after breakfast." I looked at everybody. "Now you remember. No matter what, we don't breathe a word about the Nickel-Plated Beauty. You let Whit and me do all the talking. We're the oldest."

Tom held up his hand. "I promise I won't tattle this time."

Mama didn't forget. I hadn't hoped she would. I knew her better than that. After we did the breakfast dishes, she called us all to the parlor.

"Now, children, why are you on the outs with the Johnsons?" she asked us.

"They were picking berries and digging clams all summer on our part of the beach," I told her.

"What made you think you owned the beach?"

"We know we don't own it," said Clarrie, "but we divided it up with them. They said that was all right with them, but they didn't keep their promises."

I shot her a look that made her keep quiet. Whit and I were to do the talking.

"I don't think I've understood you all very well this summer," Mama said, picking up her knitting needles. "You were always gone somewhere. Your clothes have been dirtier than I've ever seen them before, and so have your hands. I know you've worked hard. You've brought home some money, and Pa and I are proud of you, but you didn't make such a mess of yourselves last summer and you weren't so tired, either. You practically fall asleep at supper every night. What's going on?"

We were all quiet while everybody looked at me—even Whit. So it was up to me. I thought I'd tell another half-truth. "We're trying to buy things for Christmas. We've been at it all summer, Mama. We've worked like beavers," I told her.

Mama thought for a while as she knitted, but then she nodded her head. "All right, I can understand. But you could have told Pa and me. I didn't know you'd started saving up so early. I thought you'd planned to begin saving when you started cranberrying. I suppose you saw things you wanted in the wish book last spring."

"Yep, that's it," Whit put in fast, before anybody could say anything.

Mama sighed. I knew what was in her mind. She and Pa couldn't afford fancy Christmases for us. We had a tree in the house and a Christmas dinner at home, but we really shared our Christmas, like everybody else in Ocean Park, in the hall above the general store. It wasn't that the people on the peninsula didn't like nice Christmases all to themselves; it was just that they weren't that rich and they were used to it that way. When we celebrated all together, oranges and candy and nickel whistles looked fine.

"All right," Mama told us, "but don't wear yourselves to a frazzle in the cranberry bogs, do your hear? If one of you gets sick, I don't know what I'll do. You won't be picking Mr. Ross's cranberries if you're ill—Christmas or no Christmas. Pa and I can still afford a few things for you, you know."

We all nodded and began to head for the door, but Mama wasn't finished.

"From now on," she said, "there's to be no more trouble with Virgil and Vestal Johnson."

"All right, Mama."

"If there is, you'll all get thrashed. Do you hear me?"

"Virgil was trespassing in our barn." I just had to say it.

"That was your fault, really, and you know it. Meanness breeds meanness, Hester. When Vestal comes over today, you and Clarrie will show her Albert William, and you will be nice to her."

"Yes, Mama."

She let us go then, and I went to the kitchen. I had to make the starter for tomorrow's baking.

Vestal came creeping up the road about four o'clock. Pa was worn out from calling and was sleeping upstairs until supper, and Mama was taking a nap, too. All of the rest of us were sitting on the front porch. We didn't say a word to Vestal. We just let her stand there, the trespasser, while we looked at her.

"I came to see the colt," she squeaked, sounding scared. "Virgil said your mama said I could."

Clarrie and I got up. Everybody else stayed put. We walked down the steps with nary a word, but Clarrie nodded to Vestal to tag along, and she came behind us to the barn. Clarrie and I stopped at Albert William's stall. "You wanted to see him. Well, there he is!" Clarrie said.

And we stood, just staring at Vestal, while she gave one quick look at Albert William. Then she let out another squeak and started to bawl. She ran out of the barn and around the side of the house and hotfooted it for home over the dunes the same as her brother had.

"Were you nice to her—the way Mama wanted?" Whit asked us, when we got back to the front porch.

"We didn't say one bad word to her," Clarrie answered him.

And then everybody laughed. I laughed, too, but I didn't really feel like it. It didn't seem right for the seven of us Kimballs to take it out so hard on Vestal Johnson—not when there was only one of her. It wasn't fair somehow.

"I don't feel so good about it," I said after a while. "The Johnsons never blabbed about our buying a stove for Mama."

After that we didn't have much to say until Mama got up and called us girls to help with supper and told the boys to get to the evening chores. But all that next week I felt funny about the Johnson kids. Vestal and Virgil didn't even look at us at school. We really wanted it that way, but at the same time we intended to keep a close watch on them.

Miss Pitchford didn't seem to notice that things were different between the Johnsons and us. Now, since I'd been so lucky with Aunt Rose and Uncle Ced, I decided that I'd take a hand in her troubles. I was glad that Mr. Willard was smitten with Essie Akerman. That sure got the storekeeper out of Miss Pitchford's life, and I hoped he kept out. But it was terrible to think that now the prettiest single lady on the whole peninsula didn't have a beau. I hounded Pa to find out if any new men had come to Ocean Park or Nahcotta, but he got tired of it and asked me if *I* was looking for a beau. I wasn't, so I gave up on it for a while. It looked as though I'd need a real miracle for our teacher, anyway. Maybe some man would come up out of the ocean the way people did in fairy tales.

The cranberries were a little late that year. They got ripe early in October. We were at Mr. Ross's bog at eight o'clock the first possible Saturday morning. If we worked hard, we'd have the eight dollars we needed pretty soon.

Mr. Ross gave us buckets and let us go. We started up a row of cranberries. It was the hardest work I'd ever done. The cranberries, which were red and hard as marbles, grew on low dark green plants. It was easy to see the berries, but after a while the picking began to hurt our fingers. It was hardest of all on our backs and knees. The bog was squishy wet, that was what cranberries liked, and it soaked through a dress and a petticoat and stockings. Soon Anna and Clarrie said their knees were getting sore. Mine weren't yet—I had calluses on them from scrubbing the kitchen floor at the Palace Hotel.

Sarah got tired almost right off the bat. She sat down in the middle of our row and threw cranberries at Tom. Sarah didn't keep her mind on things very well yet, so we sent her home to Mama.

We kept at it, though, that Saturday and the next. Then disaster struck! It came on the second Sunday in October. Saturday night Tom had said that his knees were hurting. We all took a look and saw some red bumps on them, but that was all.

Whit said that most of that night Tom tossed around in bed. Then at Sunday breakfast Clarrie and Anna got to the table late, which wasn't like them. They walked sort of funny—not the way a person walks bent over when his back is aching, but stiff-legged, as though their legs hurt. They didn't have their stockings on, either, the way they usually did on Sunday mornings when the circuit preacher was in Nahcotta. We were all supposed to go to church that day, and Mama set great store on seeing us dressed right.

"Girls, what's the matter with you?" she wanted to know.

"It's our knees, Mama, they hurt," Clarrie said.

"Too young for rheumatism," Pa said, buttering a biscuit. "Can't be that. Let's have a look and see."

Pa and Mama looked at the girls' knees. "They're just like Tommy's," Mama said with a sigh. "Those cranberry bogs! I was afraid of this. The children have boils on their knees, Joseph."

"Boils!" Pa said. "Well, I guess that's what comes of cranberrying. You're lucky if you don't get them in the bogs. Had them myself once or twice when I went cranberrying."

"Ow! They hurt." Anna let out a yell when she banged her knee on the table leg.

"Eat your breakfast and then go upstairs to bed," Mama told Clarrie and Anna. "You go with them, Tommy."

Tommy picked at his breakfast, and he didn't look so good. His cheeks were too pink. Mama put her hand on his forehead. "Mm," she said, "he's got a fever, too." She felt my sisters' foreheads, but they weren't hot yet. "Hester," Mama said to me, "Pa and I are going to Nahcotta this morning. We won't be long at church. You start boiling water right now after you do the dishes. We're going to bring Uncle Alf back with us when we come home, if we can find him anywhere. You keep Tom in bed and covered up, do you hear?"

"Are boils that bad?" I asked. I'd never had one. My knees didn't hurt. Neither did Cameron's.

"They can be," Mama said. "Tom's got a fever already. That's because he's younger than the girls. I want Dr. Alf to see you all. I think maybe you need a tonic. You're all run down unless I miss my guess."

"I feel fine," I told her, and so did Cameron and Whit.

"That's only three out of seven," she answered.

She put on her bonnet and a shawl over her gray dress, and as soon as Pa brought Belinda around in the rig, she and Whit got in. I shooed Clarrie, Tom, and Anna up to bed and started to boil water on the old stove. Cameron and I did the dishes.

"How much money we got in Ginty's Hole now?" he asked me, because I was the counterupper.

"We've got twenty-one dollars and thirty-four cents," I told him.

"I don't think Mama will let us go on picking cranberries," he said. "Not anymore she won't."

"That's what I'm thinking, too, Cameron. We didn't get boils, but she'll think we're going to. I bet we'll have to tell Mr. Ross we can't do any more picking. I don't know what we're going to do now. We have five dollars and sixty-six cents to go, and I guess our cranberrying is over."

"We can still pick up oysters at low tide in Willapa Bay at Oysterville. Mr. Johns will let us bring him oysters, all right. He lets anybody."

With my hands in the dishwater I did some deep thinking. "That's fine except for one thing, Cameron. We're back to where we were last June with the clams. We're going to have to wait for real low tides before we can go out on the flats for oysters, and we haven't got a flat-bottomed boat to put them in or the tongs to grab them with."

Cameron wiped one cup over and over again while he thought. "I know what you're thinking, Hester. We could count on good weather in June and July and August, when we had low tides at the beach, but this is October, when we have our bad storms."

I looked out the kitchen window. The sky was a sort of oyster gray, speaking of oysters, but it was clear enough. "No sou'wester in sight yet, " I told him.

But we both knew we'd have one. October had never failed us yet. Cameron and I liked storms most years, but we didn't want one now.

Mama, Pa, and Whit found Uncle Alf in Nahcotta. He and his horse Rosinante came back with them, and he went upstairs and looked at everybody's knees. Then he came right down again.

"I see you have plenty of hot water, Estella," he told Mama. "Think you could spare me a little in the coffeepot? Or just heat up the coffee you had this morning. That'll be fine."

"The very idea!" Mama said. "No guest in my house ever drank secondhand coffee, Alfred Perkins."

He grinned. "Well, you see to the coffee. Hester, here, is going to be my nurse."

"Me?" I asked in surprise.

"Yes, you. Get me a basin or a widemouthed pan, whatever you can find. Give me all the clean rags you can get. Whitney will tear them into strips."

"What're we going to do?"

"We're going to make hot compresses, and I'll talk to your mother about poultices later on. You and Whit and Cameron are going to run up and down stairs for the next

166

couple of days putting hot cloths on those six knees up there."

"But what about school?"

"Whit stays home tomorrow, Cameron stays home Tuesday, and you stay home Wednesday, Hester. That's the day I'll be coming to lance the boils, if they don't break open by themselves."

While Mama made coffee, I went upstairs and found two old sheets. I carried them down, and Whit tore them up. Uncle Alf was drinking coffee by now, but he got up from the kitchen table and took a long fork. He dropped the strips of sheet into the pot of boiling water. Then he hauled out the wet steaming cloths and put them in a basin.

"Take these up now, Hester. Wring them out a little, but don't wring them out too much. Keep them hot. Slap compresses on all six knees."

"How will I know if I'm doing it right?" I asked.

"By the yells, Hester, by the way they'll yell. I'll know just from the pitch of their voices if the compresses are the right heat."

I went up, careful not to spill the basin, not knowing whether I felt like Florence Nightingale or Clara Barton. I guess I felt most like Hester Kimball, though.

Clarrie and Anna sat up in bed when they saw me. "What's that you got, Hester?" Clarrie asked.

"What the doctor ordered," I told her. "Get back down in bed, both of you. Get the covers off. It's not cold up here, and it'll be a lot warmer in a little while. Let's see your knees."

Their knees had seven bumps in all, four on Clarrie and three on Anna.

"Close your eyes. I've got a big surprise for you." I felt mean saying it, but I didn't know how else to do it.

They did what I told them, and I grabbed a cloth so hot that it nearly scalded my hand and slung it across Clarrie's knee, the one with the two biggest bumps. She let out a yell that made me jump, and she almost kicked the basin out of my hands.

"What are you doing?" she yelled again.

"Putting compresses on your boils." As soon as her leg came down, I put a hot cloth on her other knee. "There's no use your yelling anymore," I told her. "Dr. Alf says we have to do this."

And I dared Anna to say anything. She just sat on the edge of the bed and looked at me with her lips trembling. She yelled, too, though, once for each knee, when I put the cloths on. They really must have hurt the boils. My hands were burning and getting red as fire just from wringing the cloths out.

I went to Tom's bed in the boys' room next. "You'll be just fine, Tommy," I said to him. He was sitting up in bed and had pulled the covers up, so I couldn't see anything but his big eyes. He'd heard the yelling next door and he was scared. Poor little feller, I thought. "You be a big boy while I put the compresses on your knees. It'll get rid of those nasty old boils. Dr. Alf says you'll yell, too, but let's fool him. Let's show him how brave you are."

Tommy put the covers down now. He had tears in his eyes, but he nodded at me. He only let out a little yelp that nobody but me heard, and then tried to grin at me even when he was crying.

"I'm proud of you, Tommy," I told him. "That makes up for your tattling about Philip Amory's swimming." He grinned some more. He'd been worried about that.

I went downstairs for more hot cloths then. It was going to be a busy Sunday.

Uncle Alf was having a piece of cherry pie. "I guess you did a good job, Hester, judging from the yells." He shook his head. "Boils aren't serious, but they are certainly painful. Poor little tykes."

"Tommy didn't yell," I told the doctor.

He waggled his finger at me. "Tom's a good boy. I told them they'd have to be brave soldiers, and they believed it. Being brave is half the battle, you know."

He'd finished his pie and a second cup of coffee when I came down to have the third set of compresses reheated.

"Come out to the front porch with me, Hester," he said to me. "I want to talk to you for a minute."

I noticed that there was a big bottle of brown gooey stuff on the kitchen table that hadn't been there before and I made a face behind the doctor's back. It was one of those horrible beef-and-wine tonics. They made you feel sick and got you awful dizzy for a while, but they did brace you up a lot.

I followed Dr. Alf to the porch. He stood there a moment, chewing on both sides of his moustache, before he spoke up. "See here, Hester," he told me. "I've heard from Rose what you did for her and Cedric last month at the square dance. I heard how you hoodwinked her about Essie Akerman."

"Yes, sir," I said, wondering what he was getting at.

"I want to ask a favor of you," he said sternly.

"Yes, sir, what is it?"

He put his hat on now. "Just don't do any arranging for me, please. You terrify me. I see the Whitney side of the family coming out in you already. Estella seems to have escaped it, but Rose had plenty of it until Cedric taught her a lesson. You Whitney women are a caution. By the way, did you have a hand in setting up Mr. Willard with Miss Akerman?"

"Oh, no," I said. "I haven't been to Ilwaco for a long time, and I've never been in the Eagle Grill. But we Kimballs did have something to do with Miss Jenny's slipping Mr. Willard the mitten."

"God forbid!" he came out with. "You work both for and against, don't you?" He nearly dropped his old black doctor's bag. "What are you working on now? *Who* are you working on now?"

"Miss Pitchford, only she doesn't know it yet."

"Poor woman." He shook his head. Then he went down the steps fast, got up in his buggy, whistled to Rosinante, and was gone. It almost seemed he wanted to get away from our house.

I really didn't know why he wanted that little talk with me. I'd given up on him a while back.

We kept up the hot compresses, and Mama made up a strange sweet-smelling poultice out of linseed to draw the poison out. We sure got tired of running up and down the steps all day until the boils opened up and got well. Dr. Alf had to cut open two of Clarrie's, but I didn't hear her yell. I went out in the barn until it all was over.

Once the boils were open, they got well fast. My sisters and my brother came downstairs soon. They walked around sort of stiff-legged, but they got by. Pretty soon they could walk the mile to school.

Whit and I told Mr. Ross how sorry we were about the cranberries, but Mama wouldn't let us pick for him anymore. Maybe it was just as well, we decided. The weather had turned rainy and cold. Picking slippery cranberries in the rain wouldn't be much fun.

The low-tide days in October had gone by during a storm, so we couldn't go to

Oysterville for oysters, either. What could we do to get the rest of the money we needed for the Nickel-Plated Beauty? I couldn't think of a single way to earn it.

I started to worry and bite my fingernails again. Even though I took Dr. Alf's awful tonic every morning and every night, a whole tablespoonful, I was getting more and more jumpy from worrying.

CHAPTER 10

The Stranger from the Sea

Things didn't look up for us. We still had only twenty-one dollars and thirty-four cents the beginning of the last week of October, and nothing was in sight that would get us the rest.

We were all sad in October, too, when Pa traded Belinda and Albert William off for a white mare named Mazeppa. Albert William and Belinda got a good home, but just the same we missed the colt even if we couldn't ride him.

Pa said Mazeppa was a challenge. She was a fine animal except for one thing. She was a bit of a kicker when she was put in the shafts. Once you got her in there, she went along just dandy, though, and there wasn't another horse on the peninsula that could touch her for style.

During that month it rained so hard for days that we all had to wear our oilskins and boots to school. We hung them on hooks in the back of the room, and with the Franklin stove lit they smelled of the fish oil Mama put on them to make the water run off. Everybody else's rain clothes smelled just as bad as ours, and it got so we could hardly breathe in the schoolroom. We all had sou'wester hats, with brims that hung down over our necks in the back, but no matter how we walked, sideways or backwards or forwards, the water ran down our necks into our long underwear and made us itch.

Our scratching got on Mama's nerves when we were all in the house in rainy weather. She used to make us go to the barn right after breakfast on Saturdays and Sundays. I guess Miss Pitchford wished she had a barn to send us to. She got short tempered when we had to stay inside in the rainy weather and couldn't go out at recess, and she used to tell us, "For heaven's sake, stop scratching!" Everybody in school scratched. And the smell of oilskins got to her, too, I supposed. She often sat with her handkerchief over her nose while she graded papers. It had eau de cologne on it that smelled like roses.

The wind started to blow on November the ninth. It was blowing so hard the morning of the tenth that we couldn't walk more than a quarter of the way to school. I had to hang on to Sarah, so she wouldn't get blown off the railroad tracks.

"We better go home!" Whit yelled in my ear. I could hardly hear him for the howling of the wind and the beating of the rain on my sou'wester. It wasn't any use yelling back, so I just pointed the way home until he nodded. I hung tightly to Sarah's hand on one side and Tommy's on the other, but Whit grabbed Tommy away from me. He wasn't sure I could hold both of the little kids, and neither was I. The wind came close to knocking me off my feet, and there were a couple of trestles up ahead of us with slough water underneath them, deep water, too. We crawled across them.

Tall trees were swaying back and forth like blades of grass in a breeze. Yellow seafoam, blown in the wind, was all around us, and we had to bat it aside as we walked. When it got in our mouths, it tasted awful.

We made it all right to the barn, and stopped there for a breather, wiping the water out of our eyes before we went in the house. All of the chickens had gone to roost.

Our pig was hiding beneath the barn at the edge of her pen, and even Red and Jerry had gone under the back porch. The barnyard was a mess of gooey mud.

We ran to the back door, bending double. Whit jerked it open, and we all piled into the screened-off back porch.

Mama heard us stomping around in our boots and came out, her shawl over her dress. "Thank heavens you came home!" she called out. "I was afraid you'd try to make it to school and get stranded."

We were glad to go into the kitchen and drink the hot chocolate Mama made for us. It was so hot it hurt our tongues, but just the same it was good. After we had lunch, we all went into the parlor to look at our stereopticon slides of the Holy Land that Uncle Alf gave us one Christmas. That always kept even the little ones quiet. It was cozy in the parlor. Our old potbellied Franklin stove kept us nice and warm. Mama was knitting for the baby. Pa was doing some accounts about the wood for the railroad. Except for the wind whistling outside the parlor shades, which we'd pulled down in case a window broke, we almost forgot the storm.

We'd just got to the pictures of Bethlehem when we heard somebody pounding on the front door. "Now who is that in this weather?" Pa asked.

"I can't guess, Joseph," Mama told him. "Why don't you go see?"

Pa got up, and Whit followed him. In a minute they were back with Billy Johnson and Bert Hogan. Both men had their black oilskins on, and they were dripping all over the rugs on the parlor floor. Mr. Hogan had a coil of rope over his shoulder. Billy Johnson had a lantern—a storm lantern with shutters.

I put down the stereopticon viewer. I guessed what they had come for. "We need you, Joe," Bert Hogan told Pa. "There's a schooner out to sea that's in trouble. Looks as if she'll be coming aground on the beach."

"Mercy, no!" Mama cried.

"Yes, Estella, I saw it just now," Billy Johnson said. "We'll be needing all the help we can get, unless I miss my guess."

"I'll go with you," Pa said right off. We peninsula folks knew our duty to ship-wrecked sailors. Peninsula men were brave.

Whit and Pa got on their oilskins again and went to the barn to hitch the team. After

Mr. Hogan and Mr. Johnson went back to the beach, I said to Mama, "I want to go. I can hold a storm lantern."

"So can I," said Cameron. "I'm plenty strong."

Mama didn't put up much of an argument. "All right," she told us. "I guess you're big enough and old enough, and as long as your pa's going, you can go too. But you do what your father tells you to do and you keep out of the surf and out of the way. You can show your lantern light up high on the beach."

We promised, and we meant to keep our promise, too. We knew how dangerous storms could be. We hurried out and got into our oilskins. I checked our storm lanterns. They were already full of coal oil. When Whit split the kindling this morning, he must have filled them, just in case. It looked as if we'd need every bit of light we could get. Although it was only three-thirty, it was already dark outside.

We started for the beach, and it was hard going. The wind whipped the sand up so that it stung like a swarm of bees, when it didn't get in our eyes or noses or mouths. Our lanterns were lit, but I could barely see them for the sand and the pouring-down rain. I felt sorry for Prince and Maude. Even with blinkers on to protect their eyes, they walked with their heads down, Pa slapping the reins over their backs. They couldn't hear him calling out "Giddap" and "Whoa" today.

Finally we got to the top of the last sand dune and started down to the beach. The horses had to brace themselves against the wind. The ocean was black except for the surf, which was white and looked like water boiling in a pot on the stove. But it was a cold boiling. The waves were sky-high, and the sky itself was the color of the blackboard at school—a sort of greenish black. There wasn't a gull or any other bird in sight. The water was so high that it had come way up over the last high-tide line. It was throwing the big drift logs around like little twigs.

There were all sorts of folks on the beach. We saw Uncle Ced and Dr. Alf not far away from us, and in the distance we saw Mr. Hogan and Billy Johnson. At least, I guessed it was. It was hard to tell folks apart in oilskins and in the dark, but I saw their teams and rigs. Everybody was standing there, watching out to sea.

Pa yelled to me and Cameron to stay in the wagon or to get up on the dunes until we were wanted. Because the sea was running so high, I couldn't see any ship until I got out of the wagon and ran up to the top of the highest dune. The sight of her was enough to freeze my blood. She was a schooner, all right. She was coming in on the beach, and she was coming fast. I waved my arm for Cameron and Whit to come see, and they climbed up beside me on the dune.

The ship was a goner. She'd been blown off her course at the mouth of the Columbia River, just south of our beach. It had happened lots of times before.

Pa was waving to us now, and we hurried down to him. He pointed to the lanterns. We knew what he wanted. We waved them back and forth to let the men on the schooner know that there were folks waiting on the beach to help them. There wasn't anything else we could do, so we just waited while the schooner came on and on. Her canvas was sagging and one of her masts had been snapped off. She came rolling as if she were drunk, until the surf caught her. Then she leaped toward us all at once.

I prayed for her, but the words got stuck in my throat. I could see the men on the decks by now—little black things. I watched as some of them jumped over the side into the surf, trying to swim for shore. I didn't know what I'd do if I was on that ship, but I doubted if I'd do that, because of the undertow.

Over the wind we heard the schooner strike the beach. It sounded like a hundred men groaning out loud when her hull hit the sand. Then, while we watched, she heeled over slowly until her masts were in the surf.

All of us ran down the beach. We could see the men off the schooner in the water, but we couldn't hear them calling for help.

Uncle Ced was a hero. He went right out in the surf with a line alongside Billy Johnson. When a big breaker knocked them down, they got up again, standing waist-deep in the water. Pa and the others stayed back, but when Uncle Ced and Mr. Johnson grabbed a swimming sailor, they ran out in the surf and got him and dragged him onto the beach above the waterline as fast as they could. They got four out that way.

Then Uncle Ced swam out with a rope around his middle, while the rest of us hung on to the end of it to drag him back if the undertow got him. He brought three more men in that way. A couple of others made it to the beach all by themselves.

When there were twelve of them laid out

on the beach, Dr. Alf had a chore for me. He gave me a bottle of whiskey and told me to give a snort of it to each man who could take a drink. But he said I wasn't to pour any whiskey down the throats of unconscious men.

The sailors were dripping wet and too tired to talk to me. Most of them took a drink. Some of them took two. They looked awful, their hair all matted and their eyes dull. A couple of them just lay there like dead men. They scared me.

Dr. Alf talked to those who could talk and listened to the hearts of the unconscious ones. He smiled at me once, so I guessed they were all right.

Uncle Ced had brought blankets from the Palace Hotel. He gave me one when Uncle Alf pointed to a man who was lying on his face in the sand. I looked at him. He was breathing. I knew we were to take that one home until Uncle Alf came to look at him. The doctor knew we had room for only one. The sailors would be parceled out all over the peninsula, but the sickest ones went to the closest houses in Ocean Park, and ours was one of the closest.

Pa and Whit and Bert Hogan lifted the

sailor into our wagon, and I threw the blanket over him. It would be wet in a minute, but it couldn't get any wetter than he was. Then we headed for home. We'd done all we could. The schooner was breaking up now.

I took another look at our sailor. The light was so bad that I had to put the storm lantern up close to his face. He had black hair, a black beard, and darkish skin, although he was sort of greenish now. I figured he must have swallowed a lot of ocean water. He wore a dark-colored wool sweater and pants. Like the rest of the men shipwrecked on our beach, he was barefoot. Shipwrecked sailors took off their shoes to help them swim.

We got him home all right, and Pa and Whit carried him from the wagon into the house. Mama was ready for him. She knew Pa might bring a man home with him. We'd had sailors in our house before when there were wrecks, although I barely remembered them. Mama had fixed up a place on the horsehair sofa in the parlor for him. Later on maybe we'd move him. Dr. Alf would have to see him first, though. He didn't hold with shifting sick folks about much.

Pa and Whit put the sailor in one of Pa's nightshirts while Mama and I hung his wet things over the kitchen clotheslines to dry out. Then Pa came out to the kitchen, too, and poured himself a cup of coffee.

"Was it bad, Joseph?" Mama asked him.

He shook his head. "Wrecks are always bad, Estella, but the men were pretty lucky this time. We got all of them off just fine, far as we know."

"Thank the Lord," Mama told him. "What was the name of the ship?"

"The *Glencoe*. I read it on her bow. Leastwise, I think I did. The waves were running high."

"Where was she from?"

"Liverpool, England," Pa answered her. "I heard one of the sailors tell Dr. Alf."

Mama glanced at the parlor door. "Poor man," she said. "Whoever he is, he's a long way from home, I'm sure."

Pa blew on his coffee. "Probably, Estella. You never can tell about sailors. They ship out from any port in the world. Just because the ship was from Liverpool, doesn't mean he's an Englishman."

"He isn't," Whit put in, coming out of the parlor. "I just heard him talk. It was like talking in his sleep, the way Tommy does.

I don't know what he said, but he didn't say it in English."

So the man was a foreigner! I could hardly wait for Uncle Alf to come to our house and take a look at this stranger from the sea. It was just like in the fairy tales.

Dr. Alf did show up later on that night, and the first thing he did, after shedding his oilskins, was to go into our parlor and take a look at the sailor. He came out pretty soon, grinning. "I think the young man in there was hit on the head by some piece of the ship's rigging. There's a bump the size of a hen's egg, but he's got a good hard skull. He'll be all right, except for a terrible headache tomorrow or the next day. Just to be on the safe side, you keep him in bed, and don't feed him anything solid until I tell you to, Estella."

The doctor didn't put his bag down even when Mama offered to make him some coffee. He grabbed up his oilskins, which had been dripping all over the kitchen, and put them on. "Sorry, Estella," he told Mama, "I have to go over to Hogan's again. The captain and first mate are over there."

"How are they, Alf?"

"They're all right; they'll probably leave tomorrow for Portland and go from there to Vancouver, Canada. The *Glencoe* was bound for Canada before she came ashore here."

"They're Englishmen?" I asked.

"Yes, Hester. They seem to be, most of them."

"But Whit says the man in our parlor doesn't talk English."

"Come to think of it, I guess he didn't," said Dr. Alf. "I heard him muttering, but I didn't pay much attention. People with head injuries do a lot of muttering. Whit's got a fine ear. The sailor didn't speak English at that."

"What was it he was talking?" I asked. This was exciting.

"I haven't the faintest idea what language it was. I only know Latin and ancient Greek myself, and inasmuch as this is 1886 A.D., I think we can rule out those languages."

"Can't you tell from his appearance?" Mama asked.

Uncle Alf shook his head. "It would be hard to tell anything from his appearance, Estella. He's very dark. I don't know what color his eyes are. He could be Greek, German, French, Polish, or Italian. He could be anything. Whatever he is, though, he's not English or American or Canadian, unless he's a French Canadian. Well, good night to you."

The doctor left by the back door as I turned to Mama. "Miss Pitchford's mother was a German, so our teacher knows some German from her, and she studied French at teachers' college. Maybe Miss Jenny can talk to the sailor."

Mama patted my shoulder. "If the weather's better, we'll ask her to come over tomorrow after school, Hester. That's a good idea."

It was still windy and rainy the next day, but not as bad as before. While Pa took the wagon and team out to the beach to see what had washed ashore from the wreck of the *Glencoe* that we could use, we all went to school. At recess I told Miss Jenny about the sailor, and she said she'd come home with us. Living at Bert Hogan's house, where the captain and the mate were, she knew more about yesterday's shipwreck than most other folks. She even knew what the cargo of the *Glencoe* was—chinaware from England, woolen cloth, and whiskey from Scotland. I sighed. There wasn't much to salvage except the cloth, and the sea water would shrink that up. The dishes and probably the whiskey bottles would have broken.

When we got home with Miss Pitchford, Mama said the sailor had stopped thrashing around and was sleeping quietly. He hadn't done any muttering since morning—she'd listened at the door.

Pa came in while Mama and the teacher were having tea. He was looking sort of sad, I thought. He told us he hadn't been able to salvage much, only a couple of brown-colored pottery jugs, and they were so ugly he'd put them in the barn. If that was the china the *Glencoe* carried, he didn't see how they ever expected to sell them. He told Mama they weren't worth looking at.

"Why don't we see the poor man now?" Miss Jenny asked Pa.

Pa led the way into the parlor. It was nearly dark, so the teacher took a kerosene lantern with her. We all crowded around while she sat down on the sofa next to the man from the *Glencoe*.

I got a good look at him now. Although his hair and beard were bluish black, his skin had a lot of pink in it. He had heavy black eyebrows and a turned-up nose. When Miss Pitchford bent over him with the light, he started to talk again. We couldn't make out a single word of it.

"What's he talking?" Cameron asked Miss Jenny.

"It's not German and it's not French," our teacher told us. "It certainly isn't anything I've ever heard before. I don't know what language he speaks." She turned to look at Mama and Pa. "I don't know what to suggest to you. Perhaps you'd better get one of the Finns from Astoria here, Mr. Kimball."

I was the only one looking at the sailor when he opened his eyes. They were bluer than Mama's. He didn't see anybody but Miss Jenny, and she was still looking at Mama. All at once he sat up and, before anybody could do a thing or say a word, he grabbed our teacher and kissed her right there in front of all of us. Then he let her go.

"I think I'm going to like heaven, after all," he said in English, but with a funny accent.

"Who are you?" Miss Pitchford asked. She was gasping, and the lamp was shaking so much that she put it down on the table.

"Rob Roy Buchanan," he said, rolling the *r*'s. "Who are you?"

"Jenny Pitchford."

"And where do I find myself?"

Miss Jenny got up in a hurry to let Pa sit down. I think she thought the stranger might kiss her again.

"You're in Ocean Park, Washington Territory," Pa told him. "We fished you out of the ocean yesterday. The doctor said you'd been hit by a spar or something. I'm Joe Kimball." Pa waved his hand toward us. "This is my wife, Estella, and my kids. Where do you hail from?"

Rob Roy looked down at Pa's nightshirt. Then he grinned. "Well, you do take nice care of poor shipwrecked souls in the American territories, don't you, Mr. Kimball? I thank you for the nightclothes. I'm from Glasgow, but just now I thought I was in heaven." He looked at Miss Jenny.

"Then you're English, after all," I said.

He glowered. He did it well—better, even, than Whit. "I am not! I'm a Scotsman. There's a world of difference, little girl. I'm no Englishman."

That put me in my place—a little bit. "But you weren't talking in English a little while back."

He rubbed his head, feeling the bump. It must have hurt, because he made an awful face. "As to that, I can't say, but I suspect I was speaking in Gaelic. I spoke it as a laddie.

They told me aboard the *Glencoe* that I speak it still in my sleep."

"You don't talk much like a sailor," Pa put in.

"I'm not a sailor. I only took a berth aboard the *Glencoe* to go to Vancouver. It was the cheapest way to get to Canada. I was a sailor years ago for a time before I became a bookkeeper. I was emigrating to Canada. I intend to become a rich man." He fell back on the pillows, looking from Mama to Miss Pitchford. "Maybe I won't go to Canada, after all—not if one of you lovely ladies feeds me while the other holds my hand."

Mama went off to the kitchen. Miss Pitchford's cheeks were pink. She held her hands up to them as if they were on fire, gave him one look, which didn't seem to bother Rob Roy a bit, and followed Mama to the kitchen. I went with them.

"The nerve of that man!" Miss Jenny told Mama. "I'm going back to the Hogans'."

Mama had to laugh as she thanked the teacher for coming. After Miss Pitchford was gone, Mama said, "That's quite a re-markable man in there."

I went back to the parlor. Rob Roy Bu-chanan was the most interesting man I'd ever met. He talked to Pa and all of us as he ate some soup and drank tea. If he had a headache, there wasn't any sign of it. He wasn't poor, he told us, even though he'd lost his sea chest in the wreck, because he'd already sent some money ahead to a bank in Vancouver. The rest of his money, he said, he carried in a secret place.

"Yes, I found it," said Pa. "It was sewed in the lining of your belt. It's all safe for you."

"Thank you, Mr. Kimball," said Rob Roy. "Your sterling honesty, your hospitality, and one other thing almost make me decide to settle here. I hadn't set my heart on Canada."

Pa took his empty teacup. "I'll get a refill for you," he said, and stopped to wink at the man from Scotland. "And I can guess what the other thing is that makes you think of staying here. You just talk to Hester about it. That sort of thing's right in her line."

Rob Roy took Pa up on his words. He looked at all of us. "Which one of you is Hester?"

"Me," I told him.

"Who was that golden-haired angel I just saw?" he wanted to know.

"Our schoolteacher." I watched his face.
Lots of men didn't take to teachers much.
He grinned again. "Is she Miss or Mrs.?"
"Miss," Clarrie told him.
"Well then, is she betrothed?"
"Nope, she's a Lutheran," Cameron said.
Rob Roy laughed, and so did I. "No, sir,"
I told him, "Miss Jenny isn't promised. She
isn't engaged to marry anybody else."
"Ah, thank you for the 'else,' Hester.
That's fine news. I do think I'm going to
like it here. What did you say the name of
this place is?"
"Ocean Park."
"Would there be any work for bookkeep-
ers in Ocean Park, do you think?"
I shook my head. "No, I don't think so,
but Astoria's right across the river. I don't
really know what a bookkeeper does, Mr.
Buchanan, but Pa says there are always lots
of jobs open there. They have big salmon
canneries in Astoria."
He nodded. "Well, we shall see what we
shall see. Meanwhile, I know I'm going to
like this house. There's one thing missing,
though."
"What's that?" Tommy asked.
Rob Roy patted Tommy's head. "You're

too wee to know about it yet. It comes in lovely little stoneware bottles."

"Pa got something like that out of the wreck," said Clarrie. "He just told us he did. It's in the barn."

A grin spread all over Rob Roy's face. "Then this *is* paradise! I'll have to get my clothes on and see your fine barn soon."

"I don't know if Mama will give you your things yet," I warned him. "Dr. Alf—he's our uncle, sort of—said you weren't to be getting up."

"Let me speak with your mother, Hester."

He did speak with her, too. He got his clothes, all right, but it took a lot of arguing, and he had to promise to stay in bed two days more or she wouldn't let him have them.

Mama had words with me about him at supper that night. "That Mr. Buchanan is what I call a very determined man," she said. "Miss Pitchford is going to have quite a tussle with him, or I miss my guess."

"I hope so," I said. She gave me a funny look, but she didn't say anything else.

Pa went in to talk to Rob Roy after supper. I noticed that he had an odd-looking brown jug with him. He carried it on the other side—the side away from Mama.

"What's that you got, Pa?" Tommy piped up.

"Coal oil," said Pa.

But I wasn't fooled at all when Pa shoved us out and closed the parlor door. I could read faster than anybody else who had been on that side of him. The jug had *Whisky* on it, big as life. That wasn't the way we spelled it in Washington Territory, but I was pretty sure it was the same stuff. Pa had only been trying to throw Mama off when he came in, looking sad, after he'd been out to the wreck. I figured there were other stone jugs, too ugly to sell for chinaware in Vancouver or to bring in the house, hidden away in half the barns on the peninsula. But I was glad Pa had got something out of the wreck of the *Glencoe*. I sure hoped Miss Jenny would, too.

It looked as if she might at that.

CHAPTER 11

Sarah and the Thief

Rob Roy borrowed Mama's scissors and Pa's razor the first day Mama let him up. He didn't care if we all watched while he cut off his beard down to where he could shave the rest. We thought he looked pale but nice underneath when his chin showed again.

After a couple of days Rob Roy walked over to school with the seven of us to pay his respects to Miss Jenny. She was nice to him, nicer than she'd been to Mr. Willard, and she pulled down the map of the British Isles for us kids and pointed out where Scotland was and where Glasgow was in Scotland. Then Rob Roy told us a little bit about Scotland for our geography class that day. It was interesting, but not as interesting as when he took Miss Pitchford's arm to help her over a mud puddle on the way back to the Hogans' after school. I noticed she wasn't pulling away from him much.

I don't know what he said to her, but that night at the supper table he told us that he'd made up his mind. He was going to Astoria in the morning to look for work.

We said good-by to him the next day. He shook hands with all of us, and I knew that he left an envelope on the parlor table for Mama. I figured we'd see him again, because I heard Mama ask him back to Ocean Park for Thanksgiving dinner, and he said he'd be honored to come.

I told Mama later on, "We ought to ask Miss Jenny to Thanksgiving, too."

"Meddling in other folks' business again, Hester?" Mama asked me.

That shut me up, but since she hadn't really said no, I asked our teacher all by myself. Miss Pitchford said she'd like to come. I didn't tell her Rob Roy was coming, too. That was to be my big surprise. But when Thanksgiving Day arrived Rob Roy and Miss Pitchford didn't seem surprised to see each other at all. I guessed maybe they wrote to each other.

Mama sat me at table next to our teacher, and I leaned over and whispered to her, "Rob Roy isn't a tobacco chewer."

"That's nice, Hester," she said, and went on eating.

"He's got lots of money, too," I told her. "It's in a bank in Vancouver."

"Has he?"

"He isn't married, either."

"I am aware of that, Hester."

I leaned over again. I didn't seem to be getting across to Miss Jenny. "He's a Presbyterian, and he's got four brothers in Scotland. They're rich, too. They want him to get married and settle down, and it's all right with them if he marries an American."

She put her knife and fork down on the tablecloth with a clatter. "Well then, Hester, when are you getting married to him?" she asked me.

Everybody looked at us. Mama frowned, Pa laughed, and Rob Roy looked at the tablecloth—the way I did.

Later on he sang "My Love Is Like a Red, Red Rose" in the parlor. Mama played the old organ for him while Cameron pumped it. Rob Roy kept looking at Miss Jenny, and once or twice in the song she looked up at him. Then everybody sang.

That five dollars and sixty-six cents we still didn't have was heavy on my mind. It had rained off and on all through November, especially on Saturdays when we could have gone out oystering. Ever since we'd got boils cranberry picking, Mama was fussy about what we did.

The last day of the month I was out in the barn with the other kids while Clarrie milked Ginty. All of us felt sad. It had just stopped raining that morning. Everything was still wet and cold outside, and we were thinking about how little time we had left and how we'd probably never be able to pay for the Nickel-Plated Beauty.

Clarrie looked up from her milking stool. "Maybe you didn't count right, Hester. Maybe we have more than you thought. Maybe we won't have to earn a whole five dollars and sixty-six cents."

I knew I'd counted right, but if they wanted me to, I'd take out the salt sack and count the money again right in front of them. Mama was busy in the house with Sarah, who was just getting over a cold, so the coast was clear. I took the board off Ginty's Hole and got down on my hands and knees to look inside.

Disaster struck once more! There wasn't anything in Ginty's Hole but dirt! The white salt sack was gone!

I let out a yell that made everybody come running. "It's gone!" I told them. "Our money's gone!"

They all looked into the empty hole. Then Anna started to bawl. Tom began to suck his fingers the way he always did when he was upset, and Clarrie cussed a little.

Cameron hit his fist into the palm of his other hand. "I'll bet Virgil did it," he said. "He sure got even with us, all right."

"He stole our money!" Clarrie agreed.

"What'll we do, Hester?" Anna asked me.

"I think we ought to wait till Whit gets home," I told them. "We'll make up our minds then." I was mad clear through. "But don't you worry, we're going to do something."

"I think we ought to tell Mama," Tommy put in.

"No," I said. "That'd give the whole thing away. Whit's the oldest. He'll fix it." I didn't have nearly as much faith in Whit as I pretended. I just said that to keep the littler ones from crying. As it was, I had to wipe my own eyes with the sleeve of my dress. Clarrie was sniffling, and so was Tommy, while Cameron glowered and muttered.

"I'm going to bust Virgil right in the nose," he said.

"And I'll bust Vestal, too," Clarrie threw in.

We put the board back. There wasn't anything else to do, and we didn't want anybody to break a leg falling in. Later on we went out on the road to meet Whit. He seemed surprised to see us, and when we told him that Ginty's Hole was empty and that we thought Virgil had done it, he got madder than I'd ever seen him.

"Sure, Virgil took it," said Whit. "He could have sneaked back lots of times. Red and Jerry won't even bark at him. But we'll get our money back."

"How?" I asked him.

He thought for a minute. "We'll have a midnight raid on the Johnson barn."

"Why the barn?" I wanted to know.

"That's where Virgil and Vestal would hide their money, I bet you. They're always copying us."

That made good sense. Sometimes Whit did—even if it wasn't often.

"When'll we go?" Cameron asked.

"Tonight at midnight," Whit answered.

"All for one, one for all," said Clarrie.

"No girls!" said Whit loudly.

"There won't be any midnight raid then," I said, just as loudly.

Then all four of us said, "No little kids!" to Anna and Tom, because we had to have somebody to say "no" to. Clarrie and I got counted in on the raid.

I was scared now that I'd had time to do some thinking. "What about the Johnsons' dogs?"

"Oh, that doesn't matter, Hester. Martha and George won't bark at us any more than Red and Jerry barked at Virgil that time he came here to see our colt."

Whit tiptoed out of the boys' room at eleven thirty and got those of us who were to go raiding out of bed. We big ones were still awake, because we'd been too mad and too worried to sleep. We'd gone to bed in our clothes to save time, and when Mama came upstairs to hear our prayers and tuck us in, we hauled the quilts up to our chins, so she wouldn't see we didn't have our nightgowns on.

We went down the stairs with our shoes in our hands right past Mama's and Pa's room. We didn't make a sound until we got outside and stopped to put our shoes on. Then I took a storm lantern off the back porch. That was all we needed to go raiding.

"You follow me," Whit whispered.

We headed out across the sand dunes behind him, but first we tied Red and Jerry up in the barn. They fought with the Johnson dogs sometimes, and we didn't want any more noise than we had to have. In the wet sand our feet made a squishing sound, but outside of that nobody would have known we were on an errand of revenge.

The closer we got to the Johnsons', the more scared I was. This was trespassing. We stopped at the top of a dune and looked down on the Johnson place. It was all dark.

"Come on," Whit said softly. "Take it slow."

We did as he said, and went by the Johnsons' house just like the Indians in James Fenimore Cooper's *The Last of the Mohicans*.

We made it to the barn door, when all at once one of the dogs—George, it was—came jumping out from under the Johnsons' back porch and let out a bark. He knew us right off and leaped up to lick Cameron's face—George had always taken to Cameron. Martha, who was another black-and-white dog, was right behind George. She jumped on Cameron, too. He was covered with Johnson dogs.

"Get down, get down!" Cameron said,

batting at them, but it didn't do much good. George and Martha hadn't seen my brother for a long time and, judging from the way they were whining and wagging their tails, they must have missed him.

All of a sudden the back door of the Johnson porch opened, and out stepped Billy Johnson. What he was carrying wasn't in any of the books I'd been reading—not even James Fenimore Cooper. He had a shotgun with him.

"Who's there, and what do you want?" he yelled at us.

We never took the time to answer. The dogs yelped and ran off, and so did we. We lit out in all directions for home, and we were barely fast enough. Billy Johnson pulled the trigger. We heard the boom of the old shotgun; then we heard one of the dogs set up a howl. I knew that Mr. Johnson loaded his gun with rock salt. Rock salt stung like the dickens if you got it in a cut, and it hurt worse than blue blazes if you got blasted with a shotgun full of it. Right now it looked as though Mr. Johnson had peppered poor old George or Martha with it for sure.

We were over the dunes and gone before

he could load again. "You get any rock salt?" Whit asked, when we all got together again behind a dune.

"Nope, but I felt wind on the seat of my pants," Cameron said.

"We don't have to go back, do we?" I asked, not intending to anyway.

"No, we'd better not. Somebody will be waiting for us, and maybe his aim will be better next time," said Whit.

"What'll we do now?" Clarrie wanted to know. So did I.

"I don't know," Whit said. "I'll think about it. I used up the only idea I had."

"Well, I know what I'm going to do," said Cameron, his voice low and mean. "I'm going to get a hold of Virgil, and I'm going to beat it out of him where our money is."

The four of us chewed on that for a long time while we walked home. Nobody had a word to say against Cameron's idea. It was the only one we had. I wished, though, that Cameron didn't sound as if he was looking forward to it so much.

We didn't sleep a wink that night, any of us big kids, but we were up in time without Mama's calling us. She was going to Nahcotta with Pa to the general store to get some yarn for baby things and to visit Aunt Rose. She told us Sarah was well enough to go to school. I didn't tell Sarah that the money was missing from Ginty's Hole. She was too little to understand how important it was that we get to buy the Nickel-Plated Beauty by Christmas.

We kept an eagle eye out for the Johnsons on the way to school, and when we went around a bend in the tracks, we saw them— a quarter of a mile up ahead of us. Here was our chance, and we took it! They didn't suspect a thing, and they turned around and stood still for a while when they heard Cameron and Whit running toward them over the railroad ties.

Then Virgil took off, his lunch pail banging on his side until he tossed it into the bushes so he could run faster. Cameron tackled him and brought him down on the tracks. I could see him pounding Virgil with his fists and I could hear Virgil yelling. Vestal was way ahead of us. She caught up with her brother and Cameron before the rest of us Kimballs did, and I saw her beating at Cameron's head with her lunch pail until Whit grabbed it away from her.

Cameron and Virgil fought back and forth along the tracks, hitting each other as hard as they could. Just before we got there Cameron threw Virgil down and sat on his stomach. This stopped Vestal, too. She sat down on the tracks and bawled, not even looking up when we went past her.

Cameron and Virgil looked awful. Virgil's shirt was torn and so were the knees of his pants. He had the beginnings of a black eye. Cameron's clothes were torn some, too, and he had a bloody nose. It dripped on Virgil, but Cameron didn't let go of him to wipe it.

"You going to tell us what you did with that money of ours you took?" Cameron asked, drawing back his fist to hit Virgil again.

"I didn't steal your money. I haven't got your money," Virgil yelled at him, kicking his legs.

"Oh, yes, you have!" Cameron said. "I'm going to count to three, and if you don't tell me where you hid it, I'll sock you hard as I can."

"We don't know anything about your old money," Vestal called out, still bawling.

"One!" said Cameron.

"I don't know!" Virgil bellowed.

"Two!" Cameron bounced on Virgil's

stomach. He waited a long time before he got his lips set to say, "Three!"

I waited, too, holding my breath, while Sarah tugged and tugged at my dress. "Hester, Hester," I barely heard her say. "Virgil didn't do it."

"Hush up, Sarah," I told her.

But Sarah wouldn't hush. She piped up in a loud squeak, "Virgil didn't take the money out of Ginty's Hole. I know who did it. I saw him."

Sarah had a loud squeak. We all stared at her. Cameron took his fist back and didn't say, "Three!" yet.

Sarah nodded and grinned. "I saw who took the money for our stove a while back when you were talking to Rob Roy in the house."

Cameron got off Virgil and let him get up. Virgil sat for a while on the ties, rubbing his eye, which was getting a huckleberry color fast.

"Who was it, Sarah?" I asked.

"Guess," she said. She wasn't smiling.

Whit let out a groan. Sarah liked guessing games, and she was stubborn. "Now you tell us right now," he ordered her, because he was the oldest.

Sarah wouldn't have any part of this. "Nope. You can't make me, either, Whit. You got to guess who did it."

Virgil and Vestal walked away to get their lunch pails. I thought they'd go on to school, or back home to patch Virgil up, but they didn't. Instead they came up to us. "Look here," Virgil said to us. "You did a bad thing just now. We never took your old money, and we got a right to know who did take it, don't we?"

"Oh, go on home," said Tommy.

I thought for a minute. Virgil was right. It wouldn't be fair, beating him up and everything and then not letting him know who really did it. I thought I knew Sarah. She'd tell us the truth. She wasn't a fibber like some little kids.

"Let them stay," I told my brothers and sisters. "They've got the right." I looked at Sarah. She was having lots of fun. Her eyes were dancing with it. She'd keep up the game until we guessed, and maybe even longer. There wasn't a thing we could do about it except humor her.

I started out on her. I named every kid at school while she said, "Nope," or shook her head. I rattled off names that made Whit and the others gasp and that made Vestal and

212

Virgil mad—like Dr. Alf, the Hogans, Rob Roy, Mr. and Mrs. Johnson, Uncle Ced and Aunt Rose, and even Mama and Pa. After a time I ran out of names of people we knew.

Then I had a terrible idea. "Sarah," I asked slowly, almost scared to say it, "was it somebody who lives at our house?"

"Yes, it was!" She laughed at me while my heart fell down into my shoes. It was awful. One of us Kimball kids could have taken the money and hidden it, to keep for himself. I wanted to cry, but I didn't dare.

"I just got to do it," I told the others, looking everybody in the face. "I'm sorry." I started with the oldest. "Was it Whit?"

"Nope. He was working at the store."

"Was it Clarrie?" I named every one of us, including myself, but Sarah said no each time. Then I looked at the nine of us. "That's everybody on the peninsula we know, and that's everybody in our house. What'll we do now?"

"Give up?" she squealed. "I won, didn't I?"

I squatted down beside my little sister. "We give up. Who did it, Sarah?"

She pointed up ahead on the tracks. "He did!"

There wasn't anybody at all in sight but Jerry and Red, wandering around sniffing at the rails and the ties. We'd played Sarah's guessing game all for nothing.

"Oh, let's go on to school," Whit said in disgust. "Sarah's played a joke on us. I hope she had fun. I didn't."

"It's not a joke!" came from Sarah. She was close to crying—the way she was when she couldn't think of a word she wanted to use. She pointed again. "He did it. Red did it! I watched him, and then I put the board back over Ginty's Hole for him."

Red! We all stared at the lanky old dog.

"You saw Red take the salt sack?" Clarrie asked.

Sarah nodded. She was happy again. "Red watched lots of times when you put the money in Ginty's Hole. He thought you were burying a bone. He digs up Jerry's bones all the time, so he dug up ours, too. He got the salt sack in his teeth, and 'cause he couldn't put the board back with the sack in his mouth, I did it for him."

"Why didn't you tell us?" I asked her.

"You never asked me," she said, making me want to shake her. "Besides, it was a game Red and I were playing in the barn. I'm not a tattletale."

"What did Red do with the money?" Whit asked.

We all leaned over to hear what she'd say—even Vestal and Virgil Johnson. "I don't know, Whit. I guess Red buried it again. That's what he does with bones."

We all looked at Red, who was sitting in the middle of the tracks scratching his ear with his hind foot. He wasn't bothered a bit by what he'd done.

"If I could only beat it out of him what he did with our money." Cameron had a long face.

Sarah was mad now. "You can't. He's a dog."

"Sarah, didn't you see which way Red headed after he dug up the salt sack? Didn't you look at all?"

She put her finger in her mouth while she thought. "I guess he headed for our pine woods. He had the sack with him when he started back of the barn."

"Did you see him go into the woods?" I asked.

Her eyes got big and round. "No, Hester, I ran for the house because of the bears."

I sighed. There was a stand of little pine trees behind our barn. That was where Red and Jerry always buried their bones in the soft sand, and that was where Anna had told Sarah the bears lived. Of course it wasn't

215

true. The only animals in the woods were ground squirrels.

"What are we going to do?" I asked Whit.

"I guess we'll just have to dig," he said, glowering at Red first and then at Sarah.

Anna said, "There must be a hundred holes there, what with Jerry and Red digging and all those ground squirrels digging, too."

I took a look at the sky. It wasn't raining and there were little patches of blue, but it would sure be raining again tomorrow. "I think we'd better not go to school today," I told Whit and the others. "We'll go home right now and get out the clam shovels and dig."

"What about Miss Pitchford?" Clarrie wanted to know.

"We'll tell her tomorrow. It isn't as if we're playing hooky for fun. She'll understand when we tell it's about the Nickel-Plated Beauty."

"It's going to be like a treasure hunt," Cameron spoke up, looking happy.

I gave him a dirty look. There wasn't going to be any fun in it.

"I want to dig, too. I'm a real good digger," Virgil told us.

"Me, too," said Vestal.

"Well, go home and get your shovels and meet us behind our barn, and don't let your ma see you."

"Don't worry," Virgil said, "we won't. Pa would get out the razor strap if he caught us playing hooky."

He and Vestal started off for home, but Cameron ran after them. My brother stood in front of Virgil and said, "I'll give you a sock for free, Virge, if you want." Cameron just stood there. This was his way of saying he was sorry—to let Virgil hit him for free once. I was proud of him.

Virgil drew back his fist, and then dropped it. "I don't want to anymore," he said, and he walked off, fast.

We were lucky that Mama was visiting Aunt Rose that day. She wouldn't cotton to our not going to school. We got out the clam shovels and went to the pine woods. I figured we'd be there all day, so I was glad to see the Johnsons had thought so, too, and had brought their lunch pails along when they caught up with us. There sure were enough places to dig. One look around showed us that the ground squirrels had kept busy.

Red and Jerry weren't a bit of help. I thought we ought to spread out and dig, each in his own territory, so we wouldn't end up digging under somebody else's foot. After all, we had eight diggers—not counting Sarah, who was to keep an eye on Red and tell us if he looked as if he was about to do some digging himself. He did once, and we all went over, hoping, but he only got out an old bone and then expected us to say "Good dog" or something like that, which we didn't.

"You stupid dog!" Whit told Red. "You got us into this mess."

I looked at Whit, wanting to ask, "Who did?" He knew what that look meant—about C.O.D. and the Nickel-Plated Beauty—all right, so he just muttered a little bit more when he dug the next hole.

I guess we must have dug in more than a hundred and fifty places where the dirt was messed up as though some animal had been digging, but we never found anything except bones—a whole pile of them. After a while there was only one place left. That was a clump of bushes at the end of the woods just before the sand dunes took over. If Red hadn't buried the salt sack there, he hadn't buried it in these woods at all.

I called a halt while we sat down to eat our lunches. The dogs were nosing around, wanting parts of our sandwiches, but I wasn't giving any. I was a little mad at bone buriers right now. "Oh, go away," I told the dogs.

After lunch we started on the ground-squirrel holes near the sand dunes. We were getting pretty tired by now. Digging in the dry sand was just as hard as digging in wet sand for clams.

Red wandered over and stuck his head underneath the bushes. Suddenly he let out a funny yelp and tore out of there as fast as his legs could carry him. He was too late, though. A skunk walked out of the bushes as if he owned the whole world, and we knew right off what had happened by the smell.

We grabbed our shovels and began to run. Red chased after us, but Whit yelled at him and told him to go back behind the barn. Red went off with his tail between his legs. He had sure paid a high price for taking our money. We kept our distance until the skunk was out of sight and the wind had blown its perfume away. Then we dug some more. The money showed up in the seventh hole.

Whit held it up and I sat down on the sand and spread my skirt out, so he could pour the money in my lap for me to count. We didn't care if Virgil and Vestal saw how much money we had. They were our best friends again, and I was glad.

I counted fast. It was all there, every penny of our twenty-one dollars and thirty-four cents.

"Boy," said Virgil, "that's a lot of money."

"Sure is," Whit agreed with him.

"I wish we could loan you that six dollars you need, Hester," Vestal told me. "But we already sent to Montgomery Ward for a Christmas cuckoo clock for our ma. Our money's gone."

"Thanks just the same, Vestal," I told her. I wasn't afraid that the others would tell them about our midnight raid. We were all ashamed now of having been trespassers the night before.

"If we can help you out, we will," Virgil put in.

I shook my head. "I guess we'll just have to look for a miracle," I told them. "We can't think of anything much, Virge. It's getting awful late now to earn what we need." I put our money back in the salt sack and got up. We'd hide it again, but not in Ginty's Hole.

Whit and Cameron and Tom shook hands with Virgil before he went home, to show him everything was fine again between us. "We won't fight ever with the Johnsons again, will we?" I asked Clarrie and Cameron, because they'd been the fiercest.

They said, "No, we won't."

I was happy about that. Our being mad at the Johnsons had made it a bad summer and fall.

Whit ran so fast he was up in the barn loft, stomping around, before the rest of us got there. I'd given him the salt sack, and he was going to hide our money this time. We stood underneath the loft while wisps of hay came drifting down on our faces. Whit was sure doing a crackerjack job of hiding it. He had some rope, and he was tying the salt sack to the top of a rafter. Nobody could see it but the barn owls, and they couldn't get at it, not with all those knots Whit was using.

Well, it didn't matter much if we couldn't get at the money ourselves anymore. It was the first of December already. The next low tide was on the tenth. Oystering was our only hope now. If it stormed, our goose was cooked—we'd lose the Nickel-Plated Beauty for sure!

CHAPTER 12

Two Miracles

Pa took Mazeppa out in the rig on Saturday morning, and he was sure lucky. A man from Astoria, who was up in Nahcotta on business, bought the mare right on the spot. Pa got enough money to buy Jefferson Davis, a pinto horse that was for sale cheap at the livery stable. Jeff Davis was a good horse. There wasn't a thing wrong with him except that he was ugly. Pa said he'd either have to paint him all brown or only take him out in the rig when it was the dark of the moon. Just the same, we hoped we'd have old Jeff Davis for a long time.

We got a miracle on the ninth of December. After another few days of rain, it turned cold and clear. Our noses got red, and we could see our breath in the air. That night the stars came out, shiny and bright, and the next morning there was a lot of frost on the ground. It glittered like last night's stars.

So Mama let us go oystering—all but Sarah—when we told her it was for our Christmas money. We walked the five miles to Oysterville as fast as we could. It was a long walk, and when we got there we worked hard. The buckets Mr. Johns gave us were heavy, and so were the oysters. Tommy and Anna worked so hard they cried, but I told them this was our last chance. After we had the stove bought, I said, we could all sit down and bawl, because we'd have earned the right to do it then.

We worked like beavers, slipping and sliding over the green mud flats of the bay, trying not to get wet because of the cold. It was easy picking up the barnacle-covered oysters—the easiest work we'd done yet. The oysters just sat there waiting for us, but so did the barnacles. They were sharp, and the cuts they made stung like anything.

Mr. Johns kept track of the number of buckets we brought back on each trip, weighing our oysters on the scales in his shed. Then we had to quit, because the tide was coming in on us. We all went into the

shed and stood there, not breathing, while
he added up what we'd picked.

"Well, children," he told us, "I owe you
a whole four dollars and seventy-five cents.
That's a lot of cash."

I added it up, too. "Is that all?" I had to
know.

"That's it." He gave me the money out
of his pocket. "You come back next low
tide. You're the workingest young'uns I
ever did see."

We headed for home, so tired we could
hardly put one foot in front of the other. It
was cold, too. Maybe it would snow. It sort
of looked that way. Even the idea of ice
cream coming up—the ice cream we always
had when there was snow to pack the freezer
with—didn't make me feel better.

"Did we make it, Hester?" Tommy
asked. "Did we earn enough?"

"Nope." I hated to tell him, but I had to.
"We need ninety-one cents, nearly a whole
dollar."

"I guess our miracle wasn't a big-enough
one," Clarrie put in.

"Guess not, Clarrie," I agreed.

Tommy started to bawl again, and so did
Anna. I didn't try to stop them now. I
wanted to cry, too, but I was too tired. My

fingers were blue with the cold and cut in a couple of places from picking up the rough old oyster shells. I'd never eat another oyster in my life, I told myself.

We were halfway home when we had our second miracle. We heard the jingling of a harness, and along came Dr. Alf. He pulled Rosinante up with a "Whoa" and leaned over to talk to us. "Well, what do we have here?"

"Tired Kimballs," I told him. "We're earning Christmas money to buy some things." I was too discouraged to tell any more half-truths. Lying was hard work.

"Christmas is coming, all right. I almost forgot about it," the doctor said. "Did you earn all you need?"

"Nope."

Cameron shoved at me in the back. "Ask him, Hester," he hissed.

I didn't want to do it, but I did. "Uncle Alf, can we borrow ninety-one cents from you, please? We'll pay it back as soon as we can."

He touched his moustache. "Ninety-one cents, eh? That's a good bit of money."

"We'll give you six-percent interest," I promised.

"In that case, fine." He fished in his

pocket and gave me a silver dollar. "I haven't got ninety-one cents with me today. You buy licorice with what's left. You all look peaked today. Are you taking your tonic regularly?"

I nodded, and then he nodded back to all of us. He tipped his hat to me, said, "Giddap, old girl," to Rosinante, and trotted past us on the way to Oysterville.

"We did it! We did it!" Clarrie yelled, when the doctor was out of earshot.

"We got our twenty-seven dollars!" Cameron was so happy he turned a cartwheel in the road. I didn't know he had so much strength left after oystering all morning.

"We made it!" Anna said, hugging Tommy, who was bawling harder than ever—but now because he was so happy.

I stood with the silver dollar in my hand, looking after Dr. Alf Perkins. I didn't know about the others, but I'd just learned something. I felt a little bit sad when I should have been happy. We had the money for the Nickel-Plated Beauty, but we'd had to ask for help to do it. I guessed, after all, it was all right for a grown-up to help us out. Maybe we'd bitten off more than we could chew. I was sad for other reasons, too. It had been exciting, earning the fancy stove for Mama, and now it looked as if it was over, all the working and the hoping. We'd go to the general store Monday and pay Mr. Willard off and get a receipt for our very own Nickel-Plated Beauty. Maybe I'd be happier when we had it in our kitchen.

I never saw Whit so tickled in my life as when I told him we had made it. We were hardly able to get through Sunday at all. We couldn't seem to stand still long enough to eat. Mama said she couldn't understand why she had a whole houseful of jackrabbits all at once when she'd had tortoises for weeks now.

We kept our secret, though. Whit got the money down from the rafter, and he and I split it up to take to school with us. I put my half inside my dress in a bandanna. It clinked and clanked a lot when I wasn't careful how I walked, and I didn't dare do any running around at recess.

After school, while the others were waiting outside for me to go to Mr. Willard's with them, I told Miss Pitchford that we'd made the twenty-seven dollars.

"Well now, that's splendid news, Hester," she said.

"We're going to pay off the Nickel-Plated Beauty today."

"If you run into any trouble, just let me know," she told me.

"Mr. Willard's feeling good these days, Whit says. He's got an understanding with Essie Akerman from Ilwaco."

"Yes, I've heard, Hester. That's excellent news. I'm sure they'll be very happy."

Miss Pitchford bent her head to correct some more papers. I felt sorry for her. I sure didn't want her to be an old maid. I started to say something about Rob Roy, but when I mentioned his name she stopped me.

"Hester," Miss Jenny said to me, "I think you mean well, but please let me arrange my own life. Did it ever occur to you that you might be driving Mr. Buchanan away?"

I was so surprised I had to sit down. "No!"

The teacher nodded, her eyes on my face. "I see you didn't think about that. Men are very touchy about some things. If there's anything a man hates and fears it's a matchmaker."

She could have knocked me over with a feather. "Even Rob Roy?"

"Especially, I imagine."

"I promise. I won't ever meddle again. I

229

tried to get Dr. Alf to marry you, and he told me not to keep after him so," I said.

Miss Jenny buried her face in her hands. "Oh, Hester!" She made a funny noise, as if she were choking.

I didn't wait to hear what else she'd have to say to me. I got out of there, grabbing my coat off the peg as quickly as I could. I'd just learned something else—to give up minding other folks' business.

We all went with Whit to the general store. Mr. Willard was checking some stock, and he had a pencil over his ear. He took it down and tapped his teeth with it when he saw us come marching in. "What can I do you kids for?" he wanted to know.

"Turn your back first," I told him.

He laughed and turned around so he couldn't see. I unbuttoned my dress and hauled out my half of the money and put it next to Whit's on the counter. "Count it out," I told Mr. Willard. "We brought you twenty-seven dollars and nine cents. We want our nine cents back and a receipt for the Nickel-Plated Beauty."

His mouth fell open while we undid the bandannas the money was in. He touched Judge Amory's three-dollar gold piece as if he'd never seen one before. "How did you do it?" he wanted to know.

"Hard work," I told him.

"Danged hard work," said Clarrie.

"Clamming and crabbing," Cameron threw in.

"We picked 'most every kind of berry there is," said Anna.

"Hester's the bravest. She worked for Aunt Rose Perkins all summer," said Tommy. He'd have told more, but I shushed him up.

"We got boils in the cranberry bogs and barnacle cuts oystering," Sarah tattled.

"*You* didn't do those things. Quit bragging," Cameron told her.

"Stop it!" I had the last word, because Whit acted tongue-tied in front of Jake Willard. "We'd like a receipt, please, Mr. Willard. We want you to deliver our stove on Christmas morning."

Mr. Willard shook his head while he counted our money. "This sure beats all. I'd never have thought it." He didn't seem a bit mad, either, that we'd showed him up. Essie Akerman and love had sweetened him up more than any sugar and molasses could have done.

He finished writing out a receipt and gave it to me. Then he gave us our nine cents change. We were going to spend that on licorice penny candy and save a piece for our friends, Vestal and Virgil Johnson.

"See you Christmas morning," he told us, when we had our candy and were at the door, waving good-by to Whit.

"Just be sure you do," Cameron said, glowering, and then we left.

"You didn't need to tell him that, Cameron," I said.

"I'm not sorry."

"I'm glad you did, Cameron," put in Clarrie.

It was true. The storekeeper did have it coming. We'd paid his old storage charges extra. And they weren't fair. Still and all, though, I didn't take as much pleasure as I thought I would in showing Mr. Willard up.

We got through the days before Christmas, but we were so excited about our surprise present for Mama that we could hardly wait. Christmas Eve was as much fun as it ever was, but this year we had something even better to look forward to—Christmas morning!

The night before, all of us got dressed up and went to the square-dance hall, where there was a big pine tree with real glass ornaments on it. When the kerosene lamps were blown out and the candles lit, it was so pretty it made me want to cry. Everybody we knew in Ocean Park and Nahcotta had contributed fifty cents, so there were oranges and candy. All the boys got whistles and jackknives, and the girls got hair ribbons and pocket combs. There were balls and tops for the little ones.

It was a good Christmas Eve, with lots of kids running around the place and, later on, carol singing and Bible reading from St. Luke. Mr. Willard was there with Miss Akerman, who had on a garnet-red dress this time. Dr. Alf, Uncle Ced, and Aunt Rose sat with us. Miss Jenny came with the Hogans. I kept quiet about Rob Roy's being due at our house tomorrow—Mama had asked him.

We were all tired when we went home in the wagon to our own little tree, trimmed with a gold paper star and popcorn and cranberry strings, but we were still excited. Tomorrow was going to be the biggest day of our lives!

CHAPTER 13

Merry Christmas

On Christmas morning the seven of us were up real early, watching out the parlor windows. We didn't know what time Mr. Willard was coming, so we kept a lookout for him on the front porch after Pa went to Nahcotta in the rig to get Rob Roy off the ferryboat.

Mr. Willard came while it was Anna's turn to watch. "He's coming!" She ran into the kitchen to tell us.

"Who's coming?" Mama asked.

"Him!" Anna said to me. Anna had done a bad thing. She wasn't supposed to run up and tattle like that. She was supposed to have whispered in my ear when she saw Mr. Willard.

I went to the front door with goose stuffing all over my hands. The sun was shining, the sky was blue and clear, and it was cold enough outside to nip your ears off. Mr. Willard was coming, all right. I knew his team of black horses by sight, and I knew what was in the back of his wagon. The nickel plate just about knocked my eyes out it glittered so.

"You do what I told you to do," I said to Tom and Sarah. I hoped Mama wouldn't come out front to see, too. I hoped Tom and Sarah would do what they were told.

The two little kids ran out the door and around back to the barnyard. When Mr. Willard drew up his team in front, I heard Sarah in the back, already yelling. "He hit me, Mama! Tommy hit me in the eye." That would bring Mama out back no matter what she was doing—even if she was putting out a fire in the parlor.

I heard the kitchen door slam. Mama had taken the bait. Tom and Sarah would keep her outside as long as they could before she got around to licking them for fighting. Getting a licking wasn't part of what I'd told them to do.

But we didn't have much time. "Hurry up," I told Whit and Cameron and Mr. Willard. They'd have to lug the Nickel-Plated Beauty inside to the kitchen.

They carried the beautiful new stove in fast and set it down next to the old one. Clarrie let out a war whoop and covered her mouth with her hand. Anna's eyes were like stars.

"Merry Christmas, kids," Mr. Willard said. "There's a bag of gumdrops in one of the stove lids for you."

"Merry Christmas, Mr. Willard," I told him. "Thank you."

He even tipped his hat to my sisters and me when he left. We'd have gone to the door with him to see him out, but we didn't want to miss seeing Mama come in. We'd worked hard for months for this. And if Mr. Willard hadn't charged us storage, we'd have made it without borrowing.

Like mice in a corner, we sat waiting in the kitchen until she came in with Tommy and Sarah behind her. "I never saw such children," she was saying. "Turn your back on them for a minute—even on Christmas day—and look what they do. They start fighting!"

Then she saw the Nickel-Plated Beauty. She let out a little squawk and put her hand up to her mouth.

"Surprise! Surprise!" we yelled. "Merry Christmas, Mama!"

"What is it? What's it doing here?"

"It's the Nickel-Plated Beauty!" Whit told her.

"Where'd it come from?"

"Montgomery Ward."

"But how did it get here? Joseph knew we couldn't afford a new stove this year."

"We bought it!" I said proudly.

"*You* did? You children did?"

"Yep. Pa doesn't know a thing about it," Clarrie said, just as proud as I was.

Cameron told her, "This is where our Christmas money went."

"It took us months. We thought we'd never make it," came from Anna.

Mama sat down and began to cry. "So that's why you got so tired—you were working to buy a stove for me."

"That's not just a stove. That's the Nickel-Plated Beauty!" said Tom.

"We weren't really fighting outside. It was just a pretend game Hester told us to play. Don't cry, Mama," said Sarah.

"I think you're just about the best children in the whole world." Mama choked on her words for crying.

Cameron shook his head. "Nope, we ain't no better than the Johnsons, even if we did give them the idea, too. Virgil and Vestal got their ma a cuckoo clock. They worked, too, but there's only two of them, so they couldn't earn a whole twenty-seven dollars."

Mama got up and hugged and kissed every one of us. "I'm the richest woman in the world today," she told us, and then she went on fixing the dressing for the goose while she cried softly to herself. We couldn't cook our Christmas dinner in the Nickel-Plated Beauty this year. There was already a fire going in the old stove.

Pa and Rob Roy showed up pretty soon. They put Jeff Davis in the barn and came in the back door. Pa saw Mama's eyes, red from crying, right off. "What have these kids been doing now, Estella?" he asked, sounding mad.

"That's what they did." Mama waved her hand at the Nickel-Plated Beauty, squatting there beside the old stove. "They bought it for me for Christmas. The children did it alone."

"Well, I'll be!" Pa shoved his hat on the back of his head. "I never guessed a thing."

"It's a verra fine stove," Rob Roy told us, making us even prouder. "I never saw a finer. I doubt if the queen of England has a better one."

We nodded. We doubted it, too.

I was on my way upstairs about noon when something caught my eye outside the landing window. The Palace Hotel rig was coming toward us. To show how things had changed, Uncle Ced had the reins and the whip. This was exciting. I ran downstairs again and across the front porch and out in the road.

"Merry Christmas, Hester," Aunt Rose called to me. "We brought you something for Christmas."

"Yep, you done something for us nobody else did, and we're trying to pay you back," Uncle Ced told me.

I didn't understand. "What do you mean, Uncle Ced?"

Aunt Rose bent down and patted a canvas-covered box at her feet. There was another, littler package there, too, wrapped in brown paper. "They're from the wish book," she told me. "Ced and I sent away for them. I just couldn't keep it from Ced about the stove you children were working your hearts out for. We figured we'd like to give you something for Christmas."

Uncle Ced whipped off the canvas and lugged the big box up onto the porch, walking a couple of steps behind Aunt Rose and me. Then I ran ahead and called out, "Mama, Pa! Uncle Cedric and Aunt Rose are here."

Mama came out of the kitchen to the parlor. "What a grand surprise," she told them, while she kissed them both.

"Estella, we got a little something for you folks here," Uncle Ced put in.

"A present?" Mama said. "Oh, Rose, you and Ced shouldn't have done it. I've had my share of surprises already today. . . ."

"I know about the stove," Aunt Rose said, as she shoved the parcel she'd been carrying into my hands. "That was a fine thing your children did. Hester told me all about their plan. The little package is for her."

I just stood there, holding my package. Aunt Rose took her coat and hat off. She looked elegant. She didn't wear black anymore; leastwise, I never saw her in it. She had on another new dress, a dark-green one with lace on it the color of Jersey's cream.

Uncle Ced had already put the big package down on our claw-foot table. When all of us were standing around there staring at it, he stood up straight. "Your pa gets to open it! We hear tell Estella got the big present of the day. But first Hester has to open her present."

I took off the brown paper, and there was a dress—a pretty rose-colored taffeta. It was a real grown-up dress. I could wear it with a bustle, when I got a bustle.

"That's to make up for the dress you never got," Aunt Rose told me. I think I blushed. She meant the dress I'd lied to her and Mama about.

"Thank you," I said, as I kissed them both.

My brothers and sisters grumbled, because I got a present of my own and they didn't. They didn't understand, but Mama did. Her voice was quiet, and everybody knew it was settled. "Hester earned it, children."

Anna wasn't jealous at all because I had a grown-up dress. "Hester had the worst job of all this summer, didn't she?" she said.

I gasped. Aunt Rose got pink from the neck up, while Pa laughed and Uncle Cedric coughed. Rob Roy didn't know what was going on. Mama said quickly, "Joseph, open the other present."

Pa did. He made short work of the thin

paper and got to the box. It was made of metal, and the lettering had funny-looking words with hooks and doodads on them. He read them out loud to us:

"Die Berühmte Hofoper Spieldose"

bon

Herrn Doktor Professor Heinrich bon Kleinschmidt

Wien, Österreich

Rob Roy laughed. "It's German, Joe."
"It's from Vienna, in Austria," said Uncle Ced as proud as he could be.
"What is it?" Clarrie asked.
Pa put the lid up. It was full of metal rolls and springs and wires. I'd already noticed the key on the side. All at once I knew what it was. I'd seen a picture of one in the wish book. "It's a music box!"
"That's right, Hester," said Aunt Rose.
"What'll it play?" Cameron wanted to know.
"Lots of things, or so the wish book says." Uncle Ced began to wind it.
Rob Roy told us what the words on the top meant while Uncle Cedric went on winding. They said, "The Famous Hofoper

Music Box of Professor Henry Littlesmith of Vienna." That was all, and it had looked so grand, too.

When we heard the first notes, we all went over to sit down and listen. It was even better than Uncle Alf's watch. It played "Tales of the Vienna Woods," "The Blue Danube," "Roses from the South," "The Gold and Silver Waltz," and others even Pa didn't know the names of.

When it got back to "Tales of the Vienna Woods" again, Aunt Rose got up and put the lid down. Pa sighed. "That's sure some present. I wish we had something for you folks, but we don't."

"Don't matter a bit," Aunt Rose answered. "You already gave us a lot this year, putting up with our troubles the way you did and helping out when you could. Besides, the children are half Whitney, and there never was a Whitney who wasn't musical. A music box is cultural. The wish book says so."

I couldn't wait any longer. I grabbed Aunt Rose's hand. She had to see the Nickel-Plated Beauty. Uncle Ced tagged along, too.

Aunt Rose clapped her hands when she

saw our stove. "That's the most beautiful cookstove I ever laid eyes on!"

"It's sure a humdinger," said Uncle Ced.

Mama made coffee for Aunt Rose while Uncle Ced had a cup from the jug off the *Glencoe* and lit up a cigar right in front of us all. Aunt Rose never even sniffed. Then they had a piece of Christmas cake and went on their way to make other calls south of Ocean Park.

When they were gone, Mama sat down and asked me to burn a goose feather for her. She was feeling funny, she told me. But after a while she seemed all right again.

The goose had been in the oven a long time when Miss Pitchford came over with a holly wreath for us. Mama had asked her to dinner without my even knowing it.

"I didn't do it, honest I didn't," I told her the first chance I got.

"I know, Hester. Your mother asked me, and we kept it a secret from everybody." Miss Jenny squeezed my fingers, but her eyes were on Rob Roy, who hadn't taken his off her since she came in the door. Miss Jenny was sure pretty. She had on a blue velveteen dress with a white-lace collar and a cameo pin and coral earrings.

We showed the teacher our stove right off, and she thought it was as elegant as Aunt Rose did. As a matter of fact, all day we kept running out to the kitchen to admire it and to see if we weren't just dreaming it was there.

We had a fine dinner, even better than Thanksgiving. Rob Roy took Miss Pitchford home to Hogans' in the rig after dark. Pa said he figured Rob Roy would be a little while doing it. I understood. Things seemed to work out better when I kept my hand out of it.

When Rob Roy came back, he was smiling. Nobody asked him anything. If he wanted to, he'd tell us.

Pa took him back to Nahcotta then. I thought that was odd, because I knew Mama had planned to ask him to stay the night with us on the parlor couch. She didn't, though. She was quiet after dinner, and when she and I were finished with the dishes, she called Whit and asked him to go get Mrs. Johnson.

"Are you sick, Mama?" I wanted to know. I'd never burned feathers for her before. Mama wasn't the fainting kind.

She shook her head. "I'm tired, Hester. It's been a long and very unusual day. When

Pa gets back, tell him to come upstairs, please." She went up then. I heard her walking around over my head, tucking in the little kids. Then I heard her go into her and Pa's room and shut the door.

It was quiet in the house with Pa and Whit gone and everybody else in bed. The other kids had been so stuffed with dinner and with Mr. Willard's gumdrops and so happy about the day that they had gone to bed early without any arguing about it at all.

Mrs. Johnson came in after a while. "How do you like your new cuckoo clock?" I asked her, being polite.

"It says *cuckoo* every fifteen minutes. I don't think we'll ever get used to it, Hester. Where's your ma?"

Mrs. Johnson didn't talk much. What she said about the cuckoo clock was the most I'd ever heard her say at one time. When I told her Mama was upstairs, she went right up and didn't come back down.

"Pa's coming up the road a ways," said Whit, who came in the door just as Mrs. Johnson went upstairs.

"Mama wants to see him, Whit," I told my brother.

Whit nodded. "I'll tell Pa." He went out again.

It seemed we hadn't done much more than fan the doors of the house all day long. Pa came in like a shot, banging the back door behind him just as if he'd forgotten most of us were asleep. "I got Rob Roy a place at the Palace Hotel. He'll make the morning ferry. Rose'll see to that."

"Do you want me to unhitch Jeff Davis, Pa?" Whit asked. "Mrs. Johnson lives close enough, so I'll walk her back home."

Pa's eyes got round. "I didn't know Mrs. Johnson was here. Why didn't you tell me?" He went up the stairs two at a time. It didn't take him long at all. He was down in less than three minutes by the clock and out the back door again.

"Where you going, Pa?" Whit called after him.

"To get Dr. Alf in Nahcotta."

"Somebody must be sick," said Whit.

"It's the baby, Whit!" I knew what it meant now—at least, I thought I did.

"On Christmas?" None of us had ever been born at Christmastime. "What'll we do?"

"Wait, I guess. I don't know."

"Why don't you read to me, Hester?" said Whit.

So I read *The Three Musketeers* to my

brother while we waited for Pa and Dr. Alf to come back. *The Three Musketeers* had long chapters, and D'Artagnan didn't have any good advice for us now. I was only getting into Chapter Two when we heard Jeff Davis's hooves on the road in front of our house. Then Pa and Dr. Alf came inside.

"Merry Christmas," the doctor said to us. "Have a nice one?"

"Just fine, Uncle Alf," I told him.

"Put the coffee on, Hester," he said, and then he went upstairs, too.

Pa stayed behind. There was still some fire in the old stove, late as it was. I stirred it up and put on the coffee. I wasn't one bit sleepy. "Want me to read from *The Three Musketeers*, Pa?"

"No, Hester. I been thinking all the way back from Nahcotta about you kids' buying your ma that stove. Why don't you tell me about that instead? That must be quite some story."

"It sure is," Whit put in.

And so, while the coffee got ready, we told Pa all about how we bought the Nickel-Plated Beauty. We didn't leave out a thing— even about our having to borrow from Un cle Alf and about our being so mean to the Johnson kids.

Pa nodded and finally said, "Well, you're sure Kimballs, all right—all of you kids. I never saw so much gumption in my life. I'm proud of you. I sure am."

He got up and poured three cups of coffee. He put cream and sugar in two of them and gave them to Whit and me. "It's a sign of growing up," he told us. "Whit, you got your long pants when you were thirteen. Hester, you put your hair up when you went to work at the hotel, and soon you'll have yourself a bustle. I guess drinking coffee is sort of like that."

I drank it all, even if I didn't like it. I couldn't see why grown-ups favored it so much.

At last Dr. Alf came clomping down. He had a big grin on his face. "It's here, Joe. You can go up now. Everything's just fine. Couldn't be better."

Pa went upstairs three at a time. He was sure spry.

"What is it? What is it?" I asked Uncle Alf.

But the doctor wouldn't tell me. "It'll be your turn to go up next, kids. Right now you'll have to wait. Pour me some coffee, Hester. How was your Christmas?"

I poured coffee for him. Let him keep his

secret about what the baby was. The doctor sat down with his back to the two stoves. I guessed he'd had other things on his mind when he came in. Now was the time to show him the Nickel-Plated Beauty.

"Do you remember that dollar we borrowed?" I asked him.

"I certainly do, Hester."

With the coffeepot still in my hand, I walked back and stood in front of the old stove. I put the pot down on the Nickel-Plated Beauty, slamming it a little, so he'd sit up and take notice. He turned around in his chair.

"This is what we bought with it!" I told him.

"Great heavenly Scott, Hester, don't tell me you bought a fine stove like that one for a dollar!"

I had to laugh. "Of course not, Uncle Alf. The seven of us worked for a long time to buy this stove. It cost twenty-seven dollars at the general store. We earned all but ninety-one cents, but we just couldn't earn any more. It was sure lucky for us you came along just then on your way to Oysterville, so we could borrow it from you. That was the last dollar we had to have—the one you loaned us."

He kept on staring at the stove as if he'd never seen one before. He couldn't believe his eyes. Then he got up and walked over to it and ran his hand over the beautiful nickel curlicues. "Now that's just about the very fanciest stove I ever saw. It's a real dandy. If I were your mother, I think I'd be afraid to cook on it."

"Oh, Mama won't feel that way!" I said, laughing. But I was pleased. "Rob Roy Buchanan says Queen Victoria hasn't got a stove that's any better."

The doctor went back to the table, but now he sat where he could admire the stove. "I believe what Mr. Buchanan said completely." Now he reached into his pocket and hauled out two silver dollars. "I'm certainly proud of you children. To think you earned all that money yourselves! That's wonderful; it's remarkable. And I intend to remark about it all up and down the peninsula. This is to start your next money-making project. Here's twenty-five cents for each of you."

I figured it out in my head as I took the money. "All eight of us?"

"That's right. What'll you work on for next year, Hester?"

I shook my head, and Whit groaned. "I

think maybe we'll just rest for a while," I said. "We don't like the taste of that tonic you gave Mama for us. We weren't run down. We were just tired from getting up early and working so hard."

He laughed at me. "All right, here's another Christmas gift for you—no more of that tonic. I'll put you on sarsaparilla instead. It purifies the blood, they tell me." And he winked at me.

That was good news. Sarsaparilla tasted fine. You could even buy it in saloons, we'd heard. "There's one thing else," I said.

"What's that, Hester?"

I gave him back one of his silver dollars. "This pays off our loan."

Uncle Alf understood. He didn't argue one bit. He took his dollar back and nodded. He made me feel even more grown-up when he did that than I'd felt when Aunt Rose gave me the dress that needed a bustle.

Pa came down just then. He was smiling, and he shook hands with the doctor. "If I hadn't seen it with my own eyes, I'd never have believed it, Alf. What a day this one's been! Surprises have kept coming one right after another."

I was getting scared. What did Pa mean?

"Go on up and see what's there, kids," Pa

said. "Mama wants to see you. She's asking for you."

So we went up and quietly knocked on the door. Mrs. Johnson opened it, and we went inside. Mama was in bed with her arms around a flannel blanket. "Come closer, Whitney and Hester," she said with a little laugh. "She won't bite you."

Mama pulled back a flap of the blanket, and I bent down to look. The light was fine; there were two kerosene lamps going in the room. It was a baby, all right—but not a baby like the rest of us at all. It had soft yellow hair in tufts all over its head, while the rest of us, according to Pa, had always been as dark as the ace of clubs. Its eyes were bright blue.

"It's a Whitney!" I cried.

"That's just what your father said," Mama told us. "He said he'd never have believed it if he hadn't seen Evangeline."

"That the baby's name?" Whit asked.

"Do you like it?"

"Yep, I guess I do. It's pretty," my brother said.

I turned the name over on my tongue. I guess I liked it, too.

Mrs. Johnson made a motion with her hand. It was time for us to leave. We'd go tell Pa we liked the new baby. That would tickle him. What a year it had been!

All of a sudden I was dog-tired. The parlor clock said it was just past midnight. That was late. I stopped Whit. "We've had some Christmas, haven't we?"

All he said to me was, "Yep."

AUTHOR'S NOTE

The peninsula area of southwestern Washington State has not changed much since the 1880's, when my grandmother's family were pioneer homesteaders in Ocean Park. It is a narrow strip of sand dunes, bounded on one side by the Pacific Ocean and on the other by Willapa Bay. Clam digging is still one of the common pastimes of the natives and the annual summer people; oysters are still the cash crop.

For much of my information about the past and about Washington in territorial days I am indebted to my aunt, Mrs. Bert Soule of Albany, California. I have described my grandmother's house as I remember it from my childhood, but Mr. Willard's general store is based on a wonderful old-fashioned country store, called McCaughey's, at Bodega Bay, California. I'm very sure the old store at Nahcotta was much like it.

The fashions, materials, and jewelry are all accurate for 1886, although some of the things I mention are not from any wish book of the day. However, they are mentioned in advertisements from actual 1886 newspapers—such as editions of the *Portland Oregonian* and the *Riverside Press*. The Kimballs, Aunt Rose, and other characters would have dressed as I have described them. Moreover, the people in *The Nickel-Plated Beauty* would have talked as I have them talk, and would have danced the dances and listened to the music I've written about.

Three things are as accurate as can be. The wreck of the *Glencoe* is based upon the actual wreck of the *Glen Morag*, which took place on the peninsula many years ago. Rob Roy Buchanan also existed, although I have not used the name of the real shipwrecked Scottish sailor who stayed in Ocean Park and married a local belle. And there truly was a "Merry Sunshine Stove—the Nickel-Plated Beauty." What's more, it did cost the huge sum of twenty-five dollars, a very great deal of money in those days, equal to half the monthly wages of a working man.

Patricia Beatty
Riverside, California
November 1963